She couldn't for the life of her think of a reason why someone like Mia Knowles would have any trouble getting a girlfriend.

Unlike Eliza, who had a million reasons she couldn't date someone, and would only end up disappointing a partner with her lack of emotional availability and her busy schedule.

But something with an expiration date? A few days of fun in a luxurious resort and, perhaps most importantly, being able to help someone like Mia Knowles? A tiny spark of something that felt a bit like hope filled Eliza's chest.

"Or," she said casually, as if this didn't matter to her at all, "we don't untangle it."

Mia crossed her arms and narrowed her eyes at Eliza. "Excuse me?"

Eliza shrugged and leaned back against the railing. She could afford to be confident now. "My brother thinks I'm just a boring workaholic. And my mother has been breathing down my neck to date someone." The edge of Eliza's mouth tugged into a smile. "And you seem to have invented a mysterious girlfriend. So, maybe we don't untangle the mess. We could tell everyone we're dating for the week. Win-win."

Dear Reader,

You are cordially invited to witness Mia and Eliza's love story unfold at La Piccola Barca, a luxurious resort on the Sicilian coast. I hope the sweeping views—and swooping hearts—will captivate you.

Mia and Eliza's pretend romance unlocks a surprising and undeniable chemistry between them. I had the best time creating a romance between two stubborn women whose desires initially clashed. I can't wait for you to see how they get their happily-ever-after.

In Spring 2024, I found a social media request for a sapphic romance set in a luxury resort. I immediately began drafting, Mia and Eliza coming alive for me faster than I could get words down. I'm forever grateful to Harlequin for helping me bring these two to life.

Thank you for coming with me on this journey to the Sicilian coast. I hope you enjoy your escape to the Mediterranean Sea, where an extravagant wedding with sun-kissed days and romantic nights await.

Jenny Lane

HER FAKE WEDDING DATE IN SICILY

JENNY LANE

ROMANCE

If you purchased this book without a cover you should be aware that this book is stolen property. It was reported as "unsold and destroyed" to the publisher, and neither the author nor the publisher has received any payment for this "stripped book."

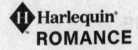

ISBN-13: 978-1-335-47054-6

Her Fake Wedding Date in Sicily

Copyright © 2025 by Jenny Lane

All rights reserved. No part of this book may be used or reproduced in any manner whatsoever without written permission.

Without limiting the author's and publisher's exclusive rights, any unauthorized use of this publication to train generative artificial intelligence (AI) technologies is expressly prohibited.

This is a work of fiction. Names, characters, places and incidents are either the product of the author's imagination or are used fictitiously. Any resemblance to actual persons, living or dead, businesses, companies, events or locales is entirely coincidental.

For questions and comments about the quality of this book, please contact us at CustomerService@Harlequin.com.

TM and ® are trademarks of Harlequin Enterprises ULC.

Harlequin Enterprises ULC
22 Adelaide St. West, 41st Floor
Toronto, Ontario M5H 4E3, Canada
www.Harlequin.com

Printed in U.S.A.

Jenny Lane (she/they) writes contemporary stories with queer characters ranging from middle grade to adult. Their stories are queer, whimsical, heartwarming...and always end with a happily-ever-something. There is nothing Jenny loves more than a fire pit, an ocean view, and a good book to read—but they will settle for any combination of these three. When she isn't writing or reading something, she works as a librarian and advocates for literacy.

Her Fake Wedding Date in Sicily
is Jenny Lane's debut title for Harlequin.

Visit the Author Profile page at Harlequin.com.

For Meaghan

When they ask me my favorite part, it's always you.

CHAPTER ONE

Mia

MIA KNOWLES STARED at the ornately carved wooden box, perched precariously on her lap, as though it contained the answer to all her problems. In reality, it held the itinerary for her best friend's wedding of the century at Mia's family's resort, the newly renovated La Piccola Barca, on the Sicilian coast. From the welcome dinner that evening, to the endless parade of chartered yachts, beachside activities and lavish nights out on the town, the event was sure to be memorialized in wedding magazines for years to come.

And Mia was going alone.

Which was *fine*. She had to do this. She *wanted* to do it. This was, after all, her best friend's wedding. And she had promises to keep. Promises she and Cate had made to each other when they were twelve years old, running along the beach in front of Mia's summer house in the Hamptons.

Or the promise she'd made two months ago, when she'd told Cate she was bringing a date to the wedding. When Cate's sister, Beth, had broken up with Mia six months ago, Cate had been more upset than both of them put together. Having a date had been a small white lie to prove she was over Beth, but months later she still didn't have someone to bring with her to Sicily.

Much to Mia's parents' chagrin, the social media influencer they'd tried to set her up with had quickly lost interest when she realized Mia had no interest in splashing her face in the news anymore.

And then there was yet another promise she'd made to her father before boarding the plane this morning. She was supposed to use this trip to boost her family's name. La Piccola Barca was their newest resort, and this was an opportunity to revitalize their brand. Mia had lots of ideas on how to improve her family's image—but her ideas, centered around philanthropy, were not what her father wanted to hear.

Mia was really good at keeping her promises to other people, not so good at keeping the ones she'd made herself. Promises like standing up to her family and asking for what she wanted.

So, she'd told her father yes and watched her mother smile in approval.

Mia shoved the memory away. "What have you gotten yourself into now?" she whispered under her breath as she stared at the box.

The box didn't answer.

The last time Mia was with Cate, they'd both been in thin cotton tank tops, singing karaoke in a private booth while on vacation in Miami. But as she sat in the back seat of the black town car, something told her this week wasn't going to hold any of those private moments with Cate that she'd always treasured.

And that was because her best friend had gone and fallen in love with Noah Brewer. And when you marry into a multimedia mogul's family, appearances had to be kept up. Mia suspected that was the reason her parents had offered the use of their newly renovated resort in Sicily to Cate and Noah for their extravagant affair.

"Mia, sweetheart," her father had said over brunch last month as he sopped up a sunny-side up egg with toast. "This is what we expect from you. Go to the wedding, chat with the guests, remind them that the Knowles family is still here. You know I'd go, but I have the meeting with the board at the end of that week. Can't miss it."

Her older brother and sisters would be at the meeting, too. The Knowles children all knew their places, and Mia's role was catching the eye of the paparazzi and media. When Mia was nineteen, they'd spotted her and Cate partying on spring break and the video went viral. Instead of her father being embarrassed, he had latched onto this angle for keeping the family relevant and smiled approvingly at her for the first time she could remember.

Mia would do anything to see her father smile at her like that again. Smiles he usually reserved for her siblings. So, she would go to the wedding, play her part and build up trust until the time was right. And *then* she would ask to work on some of their philanthropy projects. But she *wouldn't* get caught up in a planned scandal, or get photographed by the paparazzi. She was determined to leave all that behind.

Mia gently set the box next to her and bit the edge of her lip. *Think, think, think.* She needed a plausible excuse for why she had not brought a date to the wedding. Last-minute work trip? Food poisoning? She couldn't tell Cate the truth—that she'd lied in a panic. Her best friend didn't need to spend this week worrying if Mia still had a broken heart. Cate needed to focus on her wedding. On Noah.

"Just one more moment, Miss Knowles. We

are almost there." The chauffeur smiled at her kindly from the rearview mirror. No doubt mistaking her sigh for travel weariness and not the low-level panic creeping up the back of her skull.

As the car slowed, Mia took in the glowing white buildings of La Piccola Barca in the distance. From here, it didn't look like much, but Mia knew the real view was from the water. La Barca, as it was becoming known, was nestled into the edge of a cliff on the Sicilian coast. Every suite had a view of the sparkling sea, not to mention there was a private beach, luxury spa and five-star cuisine. It was the perfect spot for a Brewer to marry a Richards and get the attention they deserved.

As the car reached the main entrance, her breath caught in her throat. Being here, actually arriving at La Barca, made all of this wedding business real.

Mia took in the expansive lobby and the wide windows open to the sea beyond. It had been years since she'd been on a relaxing vacation. She'd spent the last eight years in school working toward her philanthropic dreams, determined to do something with her status in life. And she knew this wasn't exactly a vacation, but there was something about this place that felt like an adventure was just waiting to happen.

When the front desk staff let her know the family's suite wasn't quite ready, she waved off the apologies before ambling along the gleaming white marbled corridor looking for Cate. The resort wasn't huge like some of her family's other resorts—it had a certain sense of charm. And if her memory was correct, her favorite place would be just around the corner.

It was just off to the right—an airy room filled to the ceiling with shelves of books. Their heavy leather spines and art climbed the walls, beckoning Mia to come inside.

She needed to find Cate. There was an itinerary to keep, but surely, she could sit for a minute and catch her breath. She ducked into the room and ran her fingertips along the book edges. The wide windows on the far side of the room were wall-to-wall blue, the ocean staring back at her as if to say *What on earth are you doing in there when you could be out here?*

Mia was about to leave when she heard the flutter of a book page being turned in someone's assured fingers. A woman was sitting in a corner. Her back was to Mia; she was facing the sea. She had books and papers and a neat, shiny laptop spread out in front of her as she worked in smooth silence. Watching her work was like watching a synchronized swimmer.

She had warm brown skin and her hair lay

down on her shoulders in soft curls. Her suit, which made her legs look a million miles long as it clung to her thick waist and round curves, seemed out of place for a resort by the sea, but somehow it felt right. Mia wanted to take a step closer and see more of this woman.

Mia wasn't the type to check out strangers. She didn't have the desire for casual relationships that were doomed to fail before they began. Her relationship had fizzled with Cate's sister, Beth, last year when they tried—and failed—to do the long-distance thing. At least that's the reason Beth gave her over FaceTime. The awkward ending had led to even more tension between Mia and Cate's family. Something she was desperate to repair at this wedding. The last thing she needed was to get all hot and bothered by a hotel guest when she was in Sicily, thousands of miles from home.

The woman clicked at something on the computer and reached for her phone before it even started buzzing. When she answered the phone in French, her tone was clipped and polite. And somewhat familiar.

Her voice grew tense, but not loud. She spoke in an even tone and tapped her pen absently on the paper while she talked. Mia couldn't help but creep closer as she tried to parse out where she knew that voice from. She grabbed a random book from the shelf and sat in a chair near the windows.

The woman stood and began crossing from one area of the room to the next, careful to keep her voice quiet. She'd abandoned the jacket of her tailored blue suit on the chair. A soft blush camisole with thin straps clung to her shoulders, and Mia wondered where she could find one for herself. This woman was every bit the confident, well-spoken, no-nonsense businesswoman she wished she could be.

A tingle of a memory raced up Mia's spine. She knew this woman. If only she could remember her name.

The woman let out a low growl into the phone and, with one last word, smashed the end-call button. As soon as the call disconnected, she deflated like a gorgeous hot-air balloon coming down to earth and she draped her arms loosely around the chair.

"Come on, Eliza. Don't cry." She closed her eyes and shook her head, as if she was trying to rid herself of the emotion. "Not here. Not now. Just fix this."

Eliza. Eliza Brewer. As in the new CEO of Brewer Media Enterprises. Cate's future sister-in-law.

A dozen distinct moments zipped through Mia's memory. Fundraisers, parties and social engagements where Eliza Brewer was just off to the side, smiling politely next to her father at every event.

Annoyance pricked Mia's skin with the vivid memory of a few years ago when Eliza had treated her with cool disinterest at a party. And then, just two months ago, she'd helped Mia with a—situation—when she was working a fundraiser. A thrill ran down her spine at the memory of that night.

Part of her wanted to comfort Eliza, who was clearly upset about something. But Eliza Brewer wasn't the type that would appreciate being comforted.

Eliza turned abruptly and jumped at the site of Mia, clutching a book.

"I don't speak French," Mia blurted out as she rose from her chair. Their last encounter had been just as awkward. *Remind her how immature and uncultured you are compared to her, Mia. Great.*

Eliza cocked her head at Mia in confusion. "What?"

"I promise. I didn't understand any of it." Mia gestured helplessly to the phone still clutched in Eliza's hands.

Eliza's eyes went wide as she took in Mia. "Don't worry about it," Eliza murmured.

Mia was weary from travel; her brain was as

rumpled as her travel clothes. But her body still turned to liquid as Eliza's eyes roamed over her.

"Still, I'm sorry." Mia's voice was gentle as she took a step closer.

"No, it was my mistake." Eliza's warm eyes went cold, and she hurried to the desk, where she began stacking her papers and placing everything into a large bag. She made eye contact with Mia again and Mia wanted to die right there, the icy stare freezing her in place. "I shouldn't be having business conversations where someone like you could walk in."

Eliza

Eliza knew better than to be working somewhere where it could get back to her brother. He made her promise to enjoy Sicily, and his wedding, and not overdo it with work. Her mother had also not so subtly hinted that she would have a wedding date if she just "tried to loosen up a little." However, since she took over for her father, there was no such thing as *out of office*.

If she learned one thing from Elijah Brewer growing up, it was that business came first. For the last ten years, Eliza had adopted the same work ethic. The business came before personal hobbies, before friends, before sleep. And, just like her father, it also came before relationships.

Her father had learned that the hard way. Her mother left them when Eliza was only ten. It wasn't a mistake she was going to make for herself.

So she'd hidden herself away in the spot she thought she'd most likely be left alone. The gorgeous—and blessedly empty—library off the lobby.

She'd only gotten in that morning and despite her suite being spacious, with sweeping views of the ocean and the craggy rocks of the Sicilian coastline, she couldn't work there. It was too quiet and too closed off. So she'd trudged to this—not so secret—space and prepped for the upcoming merger. Her brother didn't have to know.

But now Mia was staring at her, a smattering of freckles across the bridge of her nose still making her look like she didn't have a care in the world. Her mouth formed into an O with a gasp of surprise.

Mia, who was a few years younger, and always the life of the party, wasn't afraid to be herself. Eliza and Mia weren't friends, but they often found themselves at the same events. Eliza envied the easy way Mia could move through a crowd. Eliza knew every party was a chance to make connections, impress her father and broker deals. So far, it had worked. She was just over thirty and was already the CEO of her family's company. It was worth the long nights, worth giving up any idea of a serious relationship, worth being serious. But right now, Eliza had to bite the inside of her lip to keep a smile from twitching across her lips.

If anyone could ruin her focus this week, it was going to be Mia Knowles.

"What are you doing here?" Eliza worked to keep her voice cool. Mia's face scrunched in confusion. And damn, that was cute.

"I'm the maid of honor." She said it like it was some kind of VIP pass to any location at the resort.

Eliza took a step closer and waved her hand across the room. "No, what are you doing *in here*? Shouldn't you be down by the pool, getting massages and sipping wine and taking a helicopter tour of the island?"

Mia quirked one adorable eyebrow at Eliza. "Helicopter tour?"

Eliza shrugged and let her eyes rake over Mia once more. "I don't know what people do for an entire week in a place like this."

A faint blush bloomed across Mia's cheeks, highlighting her freckles. Eliza knew she was being rude, but she couldn't help it. Her default mode was all-business, thanks to her upbringing. She couldn't just rush off to the pool for drinks in the middle of the day.

Mia cleared her throat and tucked a stray lock of hair behind her ear. "I just arrived. I was looking for Cate, actually. Shouldn't you be out there, too, Eliza?"

The way she said her name made the hairs rise up along Eliza's arms.

Eliza narrowed her eyes at Mia. *Touché*. But she wasn't going to tell her that. She didn't plan to spend this week doing any of the activities mapped out in the tiny wooden box she'd received as best woman from her baby brother. Of course, she'd attend the mandatory family events like the dinners and receptions, but she had no intention of hanging out with her kid brother and his fiancée—or any of their friends—longer than was required. It's not like anyone wanted her there.

Eliza was at her best behind a desk, in a boardroom, on a conference call. It was what her father had raised her for since birth. Her brother had the charisma. Eliza had the MBA and had spent her entire life training for her new CEO position.

She was ready.

"I was just on my way, actually. I think they're all down by the pool." Eliza knew they were down by the pool. Her brother had texted her twice, and she'd ignored both messages. But Mia didn't need to know that.

"Oh. Okay." Was that disappointment in her tone?

She was about to speak; she wet her lips and parted them when a loud squeal erupted from the other side of the room.

Cate Richards, her soon-to-be sister-in-law, stood in the doorway with her arms thrown wide. "Mia! You're here!"

She ran to Mia and they embraced in a warm hug, rocking back and forth. It was exactly the kind of hug Eliza had been trained never to give in public. Never to give at all, come to think of it. It made something twist in her stomach.

"Oh, Mia. This place is gorgeous. It's like your family pulled something straight out of my dreams and brought it to life here."

Mia waved her off and held her at a distance, taking her in.

"You look gorgeous. I'm glad I'm finally here," Mia said.

"You look…sober. Come on, let's get you settled and head down to the pool. There are some people I want you to meet."

"Sounds good. Eliza? Are you coming?" Mia turned back and her warm hazel eyes gleamed with an invitation. Eliza got the feeling Mia wasn't just being polite. There was a curiosity in her stare that Eliza hadn't felt in a long time. She really, really wanted to follow them. Her phone vibrated on the table, a reminder that she had work to do.

"Eliza, you should join us. It's gorgeous down there," Cate insisted.

Eliza thought about it. Maybe she could. Maybe once, here at a private resort, in the middle of the sea, maybe she could slip for a moment. Maybe she could try to figure out why Mia's smile was something she wanted to chase down.

"I can see you're thinking about it," Cate said kindly. She really did like her future sister-in-law. And she was from a good family. It made sense in all the important ways. But more than anything, she was happy her baby brother was marrying someone he loved. One of them should have the chance at finding love—and with Eliza's schedule and high expectations, it wasn't going to be her. She couldn't hurt someone the same way her father had hurt their mother. Better to stay single.

"Maybe this will persuade you. Mia is bringing some kind of mystery date to the wedding. And I want to hear all about it. Who is she?"

Mia froze and smiled weakly. Eliza's heart sank. Of course, Mia had a date. It made all the sense in the world. This was for the best. The last thing Eliza needed was a distraction. She'd focus on work, just like her father expected, and let her thoughts of Mia go.

Eliza nodded in clipped politeness at both of them and began gathering her items once more. "Well, hopefully I can join you soon. I just need to clean up here and get changed. But if not, I'll see you tonight for sure."

"Were you working?" Cate frowned at the laptop in Eliza's arms. "Please tell me you weren't working."

"She wasn't," Mia blurted out. "I wandered in here looking for you, and she was reading."

Why on earth was Mia covering for her? And she was terrible at it, too. It was an obvious lie to everyone, but Cate was too kind to point that out.

"Well, anyway. Drinks. Pool. Mystery date. Let's go."

"Okay," Mia said. "It was nice to see you again, Eliza."

And as Eliza watched them walk out the door, she gave herself to the count of three to be disappointed before returning to her laptop.

CHAPTER TWO

Mia

MIA WAS GOING to come clean about her nonexistent date as soon as they got to the pool. But the rest of the wedding party was already in the water splashing, chatting and listening to music. Noah thrust something frozen and pink into Mia's direction, and her ex, Beth, was staring at her from behind large sunglasses. So Mia went into charming party mode, abandoning her plan.

Mia had swallowed her embarrassment down and looked for courage at the bottom of her Bellini.

And now she was going to have to conjure that confidence again for the evening's events. There was a dinner, where everyone would have their dates and their fancy outfits and questions about her family. Mia didn't have a date. Or her family there to back her up.

But she had an amazing dress.

She smiled in the bathroom mirror and waited for it to reach her eyes. Her extroverted side was going to dazzle tonight. Her parents would surely hear about how well she'd done working the room.

She *needed* some confidence.

But most of all, she needed to find a way to say *I'm enough on my own*. To Beth, to her parents, to herself.

First, she had to get through this dinner and come clean to her best friend. She chose a spectacular emerald green dress for tonight's soiree. Her parents had offered to send her a new wardrobe for the week, but Mia had found this one all on her own.

This dress made her feel alive. It hugged all the right places and made Mia feel like she was in charge of her own life, if only for one night. The neckline was a modest sweetheart, with just the slightest hint of cleavage, and although Mia worried it was too much, it made her feel too good to take it off, like sexy green armor. She pulled her hair into a sweep of curls, added a delicate silver bracelet and dotted her favorite perfume just behind her ear.

There were many balconies on her family's suite at the edge of the property, but this one was her favorite. To her left, the sea rippled out in waves. The sunset's sherbet hues reflected in the ripples and sparkled like a smattering of diamonds. But to her right, the hills of Sicily swelled around each other like the soft curves of a body.

There was an olive tree orchard, just like the one she ran through as a child when her family visited Sicily before their lives changed, and her father became obsessed with status and the next big resort launch. Before her mother became obsessed with appearances and turning their family into a household name. The steady rows of perfectly spaced trees, thousands of years old, bearing fruit for generations, grounded Mia in the moment. She wasn't going to forget who she was, or what she wanted, even if she had to fight for it.

Her phone dinged with a message, pulling her back into the moment. It was from her father.

Have fun tonight, Mia. Please say hello to the following families. I look forward to your report in the morning.

Below his text was a picture of his favorite notepad, scrawled with names in his writing. Mia bit the edge of her lip and nodded once to herself.

Right. She had a job to do.

She repeated the names to herself as she crossed the property and braced to enter the party.

The terrace overlooking the Mediterranean Sea swirled with life all around Mia. Elegant floral arrangements adorned the terrace in bursts of white and yellow and pink. A canopy of twinkling lights hung high above them, allowing a view of the stars and the full moon across the water.

Tables and chairs dotted the terrace with crisp white linens and a scattering of fresh fruits and blossoms. Each place setting contained a handwritten menu card detailing the courses for the night. There was fish, and then some more fish and finally fish. Mia turned the menu over in her hands and sighed. She would kill for a slice of pizza right about now. She absently wondered if she could sneakily order room service later. Or escape to town for some street food tomorrow.

Probably not. There was a lot to do.

She let her hand trail over the blossoms and inhaled the sweetness of the bougainvillea and jasmine. At least there were some good things about tonight. A gentle sea breeze caught the hair at the nape of Mia's neck and her skin prickled. Almost as if she was being watched. She glanced around the space, but everyone was politely conversing as the servers expertly wove through the crowd, distributing champagne and appetizers.

Mia scanned the faces of those around her; there had to be someone her father would want her to talk to. But every time Mia glanced around the open space, the only person making eye contact with her was Eliza. Her eyes bored into Mia's with heated consternation and Mia couldn't look away. There was an electricity between them crackling under the surface from their encounter earlier that day. Mia took a step toward her, seeking more of this spark she couldn't seem to shake.

"Well, if it isn't Mia Knowles." Chad's floppy brown hair had grown into a calculated swoop since their high school days, but Mia would know that voice anywhere. He blocked her path and grinned down at her. Chad had made her days at Greenwood Prep...well, not hell exactly, but unpleasant. And of course, his family was on her father's list. "Not surprised to see you here, attached to Cate's hip, as always."

Mia steeled herself. "Chad, always a pleasure." She smiled and channeled the confidence and charisma her parents expected. This is why she was here. Keep the Knowles name in other people's mouths.

His practiced smile made his left dimple pop.

"What have you been up to? It's not too late to come to law school with me."

"I just graduated, actually. Public administration and business." Mia thought of the long hours she'd put into her degree for the last two years. The one her mother had called a waste. She'd learned so much and now had actual concrete ideas to strengthen her family's philanthropy work. There were so many potential opportunities to give back to their community. She just needed to figure out how to tell her father her ideas.

"That's cute, Mia. Maybe your dad will let you throw more parties like this one. The food is great." Chad's smile was condescending and wolfish as he tossed an arancini into his mouth.

Angry tears prickled the edges of her eyes. This was all anyone would see. It was all Eliza had seen that morning. The baby of the family—only good for getting dressed up and socializing.

She scanned the party, looking for an out, and once again found Eliza. Her eyes seemed to go right to the core of Mia. She felt exposed, laid bare. They hadn't seen each other in two months, but with one glance, one brief conversation in the library this afternoon, Eliza had stripped everything away and obviously saw the same Mia her father saw: an unserious girl who talked too much and wasn't good for anything but a party. Eliza broke the stare first, shaking her head and looking away when someone approached her.

Who did she think she was? Well, Mia was going to show her. She'd do as her father wished, but she would do it her way. There wouldn't be Party Girl Mia tonight. She was going to be polished, poised and reserved. Hopefully word would get back to her father that she could be taken seriously.

But as the evening continued, Mia felt more and more out of place. The only thing people wanted to talk to her about was her social life and what they thought they knew about her from the latest magazine article. Mia had ideas, dammit. She had a vision for her family's company. She had ideas for philanthropy, but all most people wanted to know was if she had a recommendation for a place to eat while they were here.

"Mia, darling girl, come here." Cate's mother held out a hand and gestured to Mia. Finally, a friendly face at the party. Her silver bob shone in the evening glow. Cate's mom had high cheekbones and delicate hands. Mia had always been afraid she'd crush her if she squeezed too hard.

"Hello, Mrs. Richards."

"Oh darling, we were devastated when you

and Beth ended things." Mrs. Richards sighed, clearly sad for her daughter.

"Yeah, I guess we're just better as friends." Mia said the words she'd rehearsed in the mirror.

Mrs. Richards tsked. "She was so broken up about it, too."

Mia almost choked on her drink. Beth had been anything but sad over FaceTime. She had been clinical, precise and unfeeling.

"We were quite shocked, actually. To hear you weren't ready to settle down." Mrs. Richards scanned the open space with her discerning eyes before landing back on Mia with one raised brow. "Cate said *you* were bringing someone. Where is she?"

Mia knew when Beth broke up with her, it might make things challenging for the rest of her family. But she and Cate had agreed to not talk about how Beth had broken Mia's heart. She had no idea that Beth had spun the story to make Mia look like the one who didn't want to be together. Mia felt a fresh wave of pain from the lie, leaving her adrift in sadness and frustration. She wanted to float far away from Mrs. Richards, from Beth, from every memory they shared. Fine. Beth could manipulate the past however she pleased. Mia didn't want to have anything to do with it. Not anymore.

In a moment they were going to all find their

seats for dinner. Mia knew she would be at a table with Beth and, no doubt, Beth's new girlfriend. The thought made her stomach turn. Not with jealousy, but with white-hot embarrassment that she'd lied about a girlfriend of her own.

"Excuse me, I just need to check on something." Mia didn't wait for Mrs. Richards to respond. She pivoted and walked toward the balcony as she blinked back hot tears.

The moon hung low across the water, reflecting out in long streaks of white across the sea. Mia leaned over the edge of the banister and looked out across the waves. She needed a plan, and she needed one fast. There was no way she was going to keep telling Cate that someone was coming. She needed to come clean.

"Do you make a habit of barging into people's private spaces?" The voice was low and smooth, like silk on the back of Mia's neck. The confident tone made something stir in Mia's stomach. She wished she could capture it, drink it down, give a bit to herself. "Or is that just something you do for me?"

Eliza

Eliza shouldn't be talking to Mia. She should have been out at the party, mingling, making good impressions. This wedding was a business opportunity more than anything else, and she'd been distracted all night.

Mia glowed in the evening moonshine. The emerald green of her dress set her hair on fire and made the casual freckles along her collarbone stand out in contrast. The slight curve of a sweetheart neckline drove Eliza wild. She wanted to know what was just beyond that dip.

That's what Mia Knowles was. A walking contrast. Her quiet confidence, her cutting words. Her girlish freckles, and the delicious way that dress clung to her hips. Eliza couldn't help but stare. Eliza walked away, just to breathe, to get ahold of herself. Over on the secluded lookout, the music and the party and the chatter from the guests were dulled. Her father's constant observation to make sure she did everything *just so* couldn't find her here.

But then Mia had gone and followed her. Had she followed her? Mia looked startled and kind of annoyed. She did that thing where a small line formed between her brows. Eliza spent the last fifteen years learning how to keep her face perfectly still, to not give herself away at a business meeting. But there was something honest about Mia. Eliza felt as though she could read her every thought with one look.

Still, she shouldn't be talking to her now, in the darkness of this cliff's edge. Mia had a girlfriend. Or at the very least, a wedding date, which was more than Eliza could say for herself. Just like her father, she was attending this wedding week on her own. Her father told her that she would have to make sacrifices in life if she wanted to be successful. They all had to make choices. And Eliza chose work.

Mia huffed, and it was so adorable. Like an angry kitten. "Sorry, I didn't know you were here. I can go."

"Wait—" Eliza leaned against the rail, her black tuxedo jacket unbuttoned, revealing the silky bodice underneath. She didn't miss the way Mia's eyes quickly darted down and back up. *Well, that's interesting.* Eliza dipped her voice low, "I thought this was your thing. Parties. So, why, Mia Knowles, are you hiding out?"

Mia rolled her eyes and it hit Eliza square in the chest. Eliza thrilled at the idea that, for whatever reason, she could rile Mia up.

"Not you, too." Mia leaned over the edge of the railing. The sea breeze made her hair dance as something floral and delicate mixed with the sea salt in the air. Eliza wanted to tuck that lock of hair behind Mia's ear and get a better look at her face.

Instead, Eliza walked closer, mirroring Mia's lean, resting her elbows on the railing. "Oh, come on. I've seen the headlines. Hell, Mia, I've approved them for publication. You and Cate. My brother. You are always in the spotlight." *In the very best way*, she didn't add.

God, how many times had she reviewed picture after picture of Mia for the who's who pages? Hundreds? But none of the images were as stunning as Mia now, anger in her eyes, a bit undone. So alive.

"You think you already know who I am, so nothing I can say is going to change that," Mia said coldly.

"Mia?" a voice called out from somewhere behind them.

Mia swore under her breath before she pushed off from the balcony and turned to leave. Good. Eliza should let her walk away. If she cared about Mia at all, she would disappoint her now in a small way, instead of a disastrous way later.

But before Eliza knew what she was doing, she grabbed Mia's wrist and pulled her toward the edge of the terrace. Mia gasped, her eyes wide in confusion as Eliza caged her against the wall, and hid them behind a curve of a rock.

"You're out of view," Eliza whispered. "If you don't want to be seen here, this is the place to hide."

Eliza was making all of this up of course, but dammit, she didn't care. She would say anything if it meant thirty more seconds in this space with Mia. She held her thumb at the pulse point on Mia's wrist as it beat wildly beneath her. She should shove her hand into her pants pocket before doing something really stupid.

"I *can't* hide," Mia hissed. Her breaths came out heavy and her eyes flashed with heat.

There you are, Eliza thought. Eliza had the wild urge to move her thumb back and forth right over Mia's bracelet, but resisted. It was too damn much.

"I need to be out there. I promised my father I'd—"

"Your father?" Eliza cut her off. Eliza knew what it was like to have expectations put on you. She knew how hard it was to say no to family. Hell, sometimes she was the one demanding her own brother behave a certain way.

Mia blinked and shook her head. "You wouldn't understand."

"Try me." Eliza let out a breath and leaned in close. She thought of all the things her own father made her promise and all the things she didn't get to experience growing up. Mia's breath caught and Eliza realized she would give anything to know the meaning of that one sound.

Trust me. Tell me.

"Mia, what are you—" The surprised voice cut off with a short gasp. "Oh, um, I'm so sorry. I didn't realize…"

Eliza's back was to whoever had stumbled in on this moment. Eliza squeezed her eyes shut as she placed the melodic voice. It was Cate. Her future sister-in-law. Eliza froze in place, waiting to see what Mia would do next.

"Cate, wait—" Mia rushed out. She broke eye contact with Eliza and called, "This isn't…"

Mia tugged away from Eliza's hand, her bracelet catching on Eliza's jacket cuff.

"Mia, wait, your bracelet—"

Mia's bracelet snagged, pulling Mia stumbling into Eliza. Eliza caught Mia and steadied her, but not before a small black button popped free and landed on the ground. Mia leaned down and scooped it up before grabbing onto Eliza again, more carefully this time. She pulled her out of the darkness of the edge of the balcony.

"Come on, help me explain this," Mia said.

The two stepped from behind the rocks, Mia looking annoyed and Eliza feeling like a kid who'd been caught with their hand in a cookie jar.

Cate's brows knit together and she frowned, looking back and forth between the two women. "Mia? Is this what you wanted to tell me?"

"What?" Mia squeaked.

"Mia! Oh my God. Of course." Cate brought her fingers to her lips as a small laugh bubbled out. "Why didn't I see this before? Eliza is your wedding date! No wonder you've been so secretive."

"Cate, just hang on a minute. Eliza isn't my wedding date. She's—" Mia glanced helplessly at Eliza. Panic and frustration flashed across her face.

"Oh. My. God." Cate rushed over and swept Mia into a hug. "She's your girlfriend? Of course she is. Wow! No wonder you were nervous to tell me. This happened at the Fieldings' fundraiser a few months ago, didn't it? You were both there. Oh, this is just so unexpected. I love it." Cate let out a little squeal. "Does Noah know?"

Eliza couldn't speak. She needed to clear this up. At some point, Mia's actual wedding date was going to show up and Eliza would look foolish. But Mia wasn't correcting her friend. She seemed too stunned to speak. Her mouth kept opening and closing.

Cate clapped her hands together, letting them know she'd decided. "Okay, I'm going to find Noah. If he knew about this already, I'm going to give him hell." She kissed Mia's cheek and rushed off, leaving them stunned on the balcony.

Eliza turned to face Mia. "I have a feeling I made the situation worse. Your girlfriend is going to be pissed, isn't she?"

Mia closed her eyes and fidgeted with her fingers.

"There isn't a girlfriend," Mia said as her

shoulders slumped. "And now there is a big mess I need to untangle."

There isn't a girlfriend. That tiny spark of hope set Eliza on fire as a terrible, terrible plan formed in her head.

She couldn't for the life of her think of a reason someone like Mia Knowles would have any trouble getting a girlfriend. Unlike Eliza, who had a million reasons she couldn't date someone and would only end up disappointing a partner with her lack of emotional availability and her busy schedule.

But something with an expiration date? A few days of fun in a luxurious resort and, perhaps most importantly, being able to help someone like Mia Knowles? A tiny spark of something that felt a bit like hope filled Eliza's chest.

"Or," she said casually, as if this didn't matter to her at all, "we don't untangle it."

Mia crossed her arms and narrowed her eyes at Eliza. "Excuse me?"

Eliza shrugged and leaned back against the railing. She could afford to be confident now. "My brother thinks I'm just a boring workaholic. And my mother has been breathing down my neck to date someone." The edge of Eliza's mouth tugged into a smile. "And you seem to have invented a mysterious girlfriend. So maybe we don't untangle the mess. We could tell everyone we're dating. Win-win."

Mia raised her brows and dammit, it was charming. Mia Knowles had a thousand expressions using eyebrows and freckles alone, and Eliza wanted to figure out what each one meant. "You don't have to do this. You don't even like me. I'm sure she hasn't told, like, *everyone* yet." But even as she spoke, Mia took a step toward Eliza.

"You sure about that?" she asked. "Come on, one week. It will be easy. I'll be working, you'll be busy being maid of honor. We pretend to be a couple at a few dinner events and the wedding reception. No big deal."

Eliza's heart pounded beneath her camisole and she hoped Mia couldn't see how nervous she was. Mia stepped close.

"One week," Eliza murmured. "And then we make something up about a breakup."

She braced for the inevitable no, pressing herself back against the wall.

"One week," Mia said. She slid her palm against Eliza's. "You've got yourself a deal." Her skin felt like silk and fire all at once. Mia Knowles was going to pretend to be Eliza's girlfriend. For one week.

This was going to be a disaster.

CHAPTER THREE

Mia

MIA READ OVER the scrawled numbers on the slip of paper in her hands for the third time before knocking on the door to Eliza's room. Last night, Eliza had pressed the page ripped from her planner into Mia's palm, and whispered, "Call me tomorrow and we can work out the details."

But Mia had called twice. It was only nine in the morning and Eliza was already ghosting her. So now she was knocking on her door. They needed to talk.

The door cracked open, revealing Eliza, in dress pants and a silk tank top, her hair in perfect curls. Mia stood awkwardly in her yellow bikini, covered with a sundress and strappy sandals.

"Oh, wow. You look really nice," Mia blustered. "I mean, professional. In the pants." She gestured at Eliza's outfit and bit back an embarrassed groan. Why did she always get so flustered around her?

Eliza offered her a gentle smile, the way someone might smile at an inquisitive child. Mia fidgeted under her stare.

"I'm sorry, but I'm working right now. This is why I asked you to call." Eliza's words were brusque. "Look, I'll call you later and we can meet up to make a plan."

"I *did* call you. Twice. But the boat leaves in an hour," Mia said. "If we don't talk now, we'll be talking on the boat with ten other people."

Mia didn't add that one of those people was her ex-girlfriend.

Eliza blinked at her and pressed her lips together before raising one perfectly manicured brow. "What boat?"

"Didn't you read the itinerary? Cate and Noah chartered a yacht for us today." Mia fidgeted with the edge of her bag strap. "Well, not for *us*, for the wedding party. I figured we should arrive together. It will make our story a bit more plausible."

Eliza's eyes went wide as she shook her head. "I don't…boat." She looked back into her room with regret. "I wasn't planning to go."

Mia hoisted her bag higher onto her shoulder and bit the edge of her lip. Nerves swirled in her stomach. She didn't want to keep up this charade alone. "Oh. Okay. That's fine. I can just tell everyone you're busy. With, um, work. It's work, right?"

Eliza huffed out a breath and frowned. A small line appeared between her brows and Mia had the urge to smooth it out. She wasn't used to seeing Eliza unmoored, and she didn't like it one bit. "Please…don't tell my brother I'm working right now. Just… Come in, okay?"

Mia counted the minutes on her phone as she sat in the wingback chair of Eliza's sitting area. Five minutes later, Eliza emerged from her bedroom with her hair neatly tucked under a wide-brimmed hat and wearing soft linen pants. A black swimsuit strap peeked out at Mia from under Eliza's shirt, making Mia's brain slightly fuzzy.

"Let's get this over with." Eliza spoke with the efficiency she probably used when staring down a large to-do list at work.

Mia didn't want to change Eliza. She didn't want her to feel like she couldn't be herself. But she wanted to see how hard she could push her to open up. Mia knew under that hard exterior there had to be some kind of softness.

She leaned forward and tugged on the wide brim of the hat. Eliza's eyes went wide and it made Mia want to do it again.

"Let's have some fun." Mia winked.

* * *

The morning sun sent sparkles dancing across the azure ocean, but all eyes were on Mia and Eliza as they boarded the impressive yacht, looking like a mismatched pair of socks.

"I was worried you'd leave without us," Mia called into the morning air.

Cate laughed and waved to her from the deck of the yacht. "We almost did. Get up here!"

"Welcome to *Amore Mio*." An older man with a barrel chest covered in a white polo held out his hand. He had a thatch of dark brown curls and laugh lines crinkled his eyes as he helped Mia cross onto the boat. "I'm Captain Marcello. My crew and I will take excellent care of you today."

"It seems you already are," Mia said with a broad smile. "Thank you for waiting for us."

"My pleasure, signorina." He turned to Eliza, who did not take his hand and boarded the boat with confidence and the air of someone who just wanted to get this over with.

The ship was a substantial sixty feet at least, and as they made their way to the front they found fresh fruits, pastries and, yet again, fish, laid out in a massive charcuterie spread. A bar sat off to one side with a young man in a crisp blue polo waiting to serve them.

Beth sat in a lounger at the edge of the deck.

Which Mia expected. Of course Beth would be there. She was part of the wedding party. But her girlfriend wasn't with her, which Mia had to admit was a bit of a relief.

"Remember," Cate said as she held up something alcoholic and fruity. "This is a relaxation zone. A time for us to unwind away from our families before things get hectic this week."

Everyone collectively nodded and whooped while Noah scooped Cate into his arms and carried her off somewhere secluded as they prepared to leave the harbor.

Two of Noah's groomsmen gathered near the bar, already ordering drinks. Eliza wandered over to the edge of the deck, leaning over the railing and staring out into the cerulean water, her ridiculous wide-brimmed hat obscuring her face.

Mia's stomach swooped. She thought she was going to spend today relaxing, but one look at Eliza and her entire body felt like a firework about to go off. She dropped her bag near a chair, abandoning her book and sweater, and headed to the edge of the deck.

"Hey," Mia said gently, not wanting to spook Eliza. "Is now a good time to figure some things out?"

"What is there to figure out?" Eliza stiffened, but then forced her shoulders to relax. "We're on a boat. We…do boat things."

Beth shuffled a few feet away, clearly trying to listen in on their conversation. Like hell was Mia going to let that happen.

"Yes, but we're going to have to do them as a couple," Mia hissed into Eliza's ear. She glared at her meaningfully and Eliza sighed.

Eliza slid her hand into Mia's and squeezed. "Come on, babe," she said over her shoulder. Mia followed her gaze to find several people watching them. "I want to explore this boat."

Eliza kept Mia's hand in hers and led her up a series of stairs to the top of the yacht. It was windy up there, loud in a way that centered her and calmed her nerves. Eliza dropped her hand as soon as they were out of view. Mia leaned over the railing and frowned. Had she done something wrong?

"I'm already messing this up, aren't I?" Mia sighed. "I'm sorry, I've just never done this before, and I want to be good and I... I don't know how."

Eliza's frown deepened and she huffed out a breath. "Mia, you aren't doing anything wrong." Eliza grabbed Mia's shoulders and Mia felt it everywhere. The slight brush of her thumbs on the edge of her bikini strap, the firm pressure of her palms against Mia's cool skin.

"You're just saying that." Mia sighed. "I know how to *turn it on* when it's expected. I know how to charm a room and be the life of the party, but for some reason, I'm off my game. And you're giving up so much to be here. I know you wish you were working."

"For the record, you're making me say this." Eliza's voice shifted into what Mia imagined she sounded like in a boardroom. "You are Mia Knowles. You are smart and creative and brave. You have a master's degree. And I know what I signed up for. My work won't suffer, because my work *never* suffers. And this?" She gestured vaguely between the two of them with her free hand. "This is going to be fine."

The words rushed over Mia like a burst of sunlight peeking through clouds. Eliza must have noticed she was touching Mia with no one watching, because she removed her hands quickly and cleared her throat.

"You know about my master's?" Mia asked.

"Oh." Eliza shifted her eyes and looked away. "You mentioned it at that party a couple months ago. And I think my brother told me. Anyway—" she squared her shoulders and smiled "—we don't need some scheme. We just tell the truth as much as possible. So, let's go downstairs and wow them at breakfast. We've got this."

But ten minutes into breakfast, Mia realized she did not totally have this. And neither did Eliza. For all her confidence, when Noah asked his sister why they bothered with separate rooms, she practically spit her mimosa across the table. And while Eliza always seemed in control, this morning her leg danced under the table in a slight tap with each new question.

"I'm just saying." Noah shrugged and took another bite of his omelet. "I'm sure we can move you into the same room."

"That's not necessary," Eliza said with a shrug. "We didn't want to draw attention to us and take away from your big day."

"I'm staying in the family suite," Mia blurted out. As if that explained everything. She felt every bit the stereotype of a spoiled heiress that she was working so hard to combat. "My parents insisted."

"And I know Mia likes her early-morning runs." Eliza shrugged and took a sip of mimosa. "She needed at least one night of rest."

How on earth could Eliza know that? Did something about Mia scream runner?

"Mia, you went for a run?" Cate pouted. "But this is my wedding week. Relaxation only!"

"Running is relaxing. For me."

The conversation shifted into a debate of the best trails to run, then the best golf courses to play on, and Mia turned to face Eliza. Eliza's deep brown eyes stared back at her.

"How did you know?" she mouthed at Eliza. "About the running?"

"I saw you," she murmured noncommittally. Eliza leaned in close, her breath hot against Mia's ear. It tickled her neck, and she laughed despite herself. Mia didn't turn. She didn't dare move an inch. Eliza's nose ran along the shell of her ear and she wasn't sure if it was an accident or an act. Either way, she reminded herself not to get too carried away.

"You saw me?" Mia's voice was barely a breath. She grasped her water glass, but it was sweating and her fingers slipped.

"Running along the beach this morning. Do you always run barefoot?" Eliza said the word *barefoot* like it meant naked. And it might as well have the way Mia shivered.

Eliza

When Noah asked Eliza to be his best woman, she figured her duties would include standing beside him on his wedding day and giving a toast. She was good at giving speeches and rarely minded being scrutinized by groups, so she'd said yes.

There was also the fact that she loved her baby brother more than anything in the world. Even if she hadn't always done a good job of showing it. Especially in the last few years. But upon her arrival in Sicily, she'd been gifted an ornate wooden box with five days' worth of events for the wedding party outlined on heavy white paper inside.

She'd planned to skip every single one. Her father made sure she understood how demanding her new role as CEO would be—and she intended to make him proud. She'd been working eighteen-hour days. Sometimes longer. And just because she was in Sicily for the week, that didn't mean the work stopped. Even now, there were a million tasks she was ignoring to be here.

It was around four o'clock that morning that she bolted upright in bed. She'd forgotten to send notes to her administrative assistant before falling asleep. She *never* forgot to send notes before going to sleep. How could she have been so irresponsible?

It's not like she could make this up later. Promising to fake date Mia meant she had to attend this barrage of events. Her pulse raced, and it took another twenty minutes of tossing and turning to admit sleep would not happen if she didn't get some work done first.

She'd pulled herself from the bed, made a cup of coffee and thrown open her windows. The sky was the perfect shade of dusky gray blue you only see when night meets morning, and the world was calm. It was Eliza's favorite time of day. When the world was still and her brain had space to spread out. The breeze billowed the curtains, calling her to the window.

And there, down below, a mile away, a woman was running on the beach, right where water met sand. A fire-red ponytail dark in the moonlight swished back and forth. She couldn't see her face, but it had to be Mia. Seeing her doing something she clearly loved, something just for her, had made Eliza's whole chest ache.

And now that woman was lying next to her on a lounge chair, after the world's most awkward breakfast. Eliza could count eleven freckles along her waist from behind her sunglasses.

Mia had been ridiculous at breakfast, blushing beautifully whenever Eliza got within six inches of her. After that, the entire bridal party had spent the rest of the morning swimming and looking at the sea life around them.

Eliza spent the morning trying not to focus too much on Mia. The way her hair fanned out behind her in the water like fireworks. The way she'd blow out a long string of bubbles when she spotted sea life, as if she couldn't contain her joy. How water would bead across her chest when she pulled herself up on the ladder.

It was hard to reconcile the woman running on the beach with the woman Eliza had sat beside at breakfast. Surely, the awkward, blushing woman couldn't be the same as the confident one so in her element running along the shore? But it didn't matter now; they'd made it through the meal and the swimming afterward. What was much more pressing now was Mia laid out on her lounge chair, her sundress and towel discarded on the deck beside her. Eliza named each magazine category she oversaw, in alphabetical order, to keep her from saying something stupid.

Mia pulled her hair to one side and sighed. Twelve freckles. There was one on the slope of her shoulder near her neck. Eliza's throat went dry.

The second Noah and his friends had convinced a steward to let them try out the Jet Skis, Cate sat up straight and pointed a finger between the two of them.

"Okay, Mia. Spill it. How did the two of you get together?"

They'd successfully avoided this topic all morning and Eliza had foolishly assumed they would have time to work this out before they had to answer.

"Yeah, Mia. I'm sure there's a story there." Beth sat in the shade under the awning. Her words were saccharine sweet as she clicked a button to turn the page on her e-reader and frowned. "Why don't you tell us all about it?"

Eliza didn't miss the way Mia stiffened at Beth's words. She knew they had a history, but she didn't know how the two had ended things. She added it to the list of one million things she didn't know about Mia Knowles, but was determined to find out.

Mia turned her head toward Eliza and her eyes went wide. She was up to something.

"Go on, babe, tell them." Mia smiled at Eliza and bit her tongue between her teeth. "It's so much better when you tell it."

Eliza ignored how cute Mia looked with her tongue poking out. Mia Knowles was trouble. But when Mia crinkled her nose, Eliza rolled her eyes and said without thinking, "I've always had a thing for Mia."

"What?" Cate's voice was a high squeak.

To Mia's credit, she didn't balk. Her eyes narrowed and she pressed her lips together in a smile.

"Of course. Look at her. She's amazing. But it was two months ago that we finally talked." Eliza didn't realize she was going to tell this story until it was tumbling out. "You were right, Cate. It was at the Fieldings' fundraiser. Mia helped organize the donor recognitions. She was so…competent. She had this clipboard and kept biting her pencil. It was the hottest damn thing

I'd seen in my life. So I made sure we bumped into each other and I offered to help."

Eliza's cheeks were on fire as she looked Mia in the eyes and said, "And I haven't stopped falling since."

Mia's gaze turned heated and her eyes went wide for a moment before she schooled her features. Eliza was in trouble. She knew it. Because Mia remembered. She remembered that night, too.

And Eliza was terrified Mia might know that she was actually telling the truth.

CHAPTER FOUR

Mia

MIA'S STOMACH FIZZED with anticipation as a candy-apple-red cable car came careening around the bend. It swayed back and forth from the momentum as a worker grabbed onto the rail and pulled it to a crawl. Exploring Mount Etna had been on her bucket list for as long as she could remember, and the impending cable car ride was a nice distraction from the butterflies in her stomach at the idea of seeing Eliza again today.

Of *pretending* again today.

"Do you want to ride with us?" Cate said, gesturing toward the car. "Noah and I don't mind."

The rest of the party had already climbed into the earlier cars, but Mia stalled as long as she could. Not because she was scared, but because Eliza hadn't shown up yet. Maybe she would not come at all.

But just then, a town car pulled up. The driver quickly rounded the front of the car and opened the passenger door, revealing a pair of long legs, then wide hips, and finally a waist that curved in slightly. Mia's throat went dry.

"Oh, good. She made it." Noah seemed just as surprised as Mia felt. "We'll see you up there, okay?" And with that, he and Cate jumped into the waiting cable car.

It was one thing to pretend to be together while people were watching. It was another to be trapped with Eliza Brewer for fifteen minutes as they ascended a mountain with nothing to talk about. Because Mia was not going to bring up the bomb Eliza had dropped yesterday on the yacht when she mentioned the Fieldings' fundraiser.

Mia had spent the last two months trying to forget the night that ended in disappointment. She'd been so excited when Mrs. Fielding had approached her with an opportunity to get involved. The weeks she'd spent working on the team and preparing for the fundraiser behind her parents' backs had been exhilarating. She'd shoved that night—and the woman who was the one bright spot of her evening before it fell apart—deep down in a locked box of her heart.

Mia had worn a simple black dress with a suit coat and had kept her hair up and out of her face in order to stay focused the entire afternoon. Her weeks of hard work had paid off. Donors had seemed happy, champagne had been flowing and, so far, her parents had not noticed that Mia had been working at the event instead of attending it.

In a few moments, she would change into something more acceptable for a Knowles, tug her hair down and join her family.

She would show them her work, her involvement. Her father was going to be impressed. This was going to work. He would have no choice but to allow her to support the family's philanthropic efforts. He would have to give her a rightful spot in the company.

She had bitten the edge of a pencil, a terrible habit she needed to break, and checked the last name off the list before dropping her clipboard on the table. She had glanced around the hall and noticed her parents chatting with another couple across the room. Panic had filled her chest as they began walking. If her parents saw her like this, well, her secret would be out.

Mia had dashed toward the room where she had stored her second dress and quickly removed the silver-sequined number from a garment bag, nearly tripping in her hurry to pull it up her body. Her elbow had banged against the edge of a chair as she had attempted to pull up the zipper.

No matter, she had decided—she would just finish it up in front of the mirror.

Once she had adjusted the dress, she had attempted the zipper again. But the zipper had been stuck, leaving her breasts exposed in the front. She was going to have to walk out of this room with a wardrobe malfunction to flag down someone on the staff. With her luck, someone would catch it on camera, and the only thing her family would remember from this night would be how Mia Knowles had been in the news again.

"No, no, no," she had muttered as she desperately tried to reach the zipper behind her. "Come on, stupid zipper."

She had tugged again, to no avail. The zipper had been caught on itself, and no matter how hard she tugged, it hadn't budged. Tears had pricked her eyes. How had she thought she could pull this off? If she couldn't change, then she would have to put her suit back on, and that wouldn't do for her father.

She had searched the room for something she could use to zip the dress. A hook maybe? The edge of a hanger? The door had clicked open, and Mia had frozen, casting her eyes downward.

She hadn't wanted anyone to see her with half her chest hanging out.

"Oh! I'm so sorry, I thought this was the restroom." The woman had averted her eyes. Mia had waited for her to leave, but she had taken a step closer and said, "Hmm…looks like you could use some help. May I?"

Mia had nodded. "That would be great. Thank you, it's just… I can't let my parents see me like this. I'm not supposed to be working, but I was working, and now I'm not going to be able to go out there," she had rambled. "I'm supposed to be out there, dazzling people. But I can't do that with…" Mia had made a vague gesture at her chest.

"You're going to have to turn around."

Mia had finally looked up, noting the amusement dancing in the woman's eyes. Mia let out a small gasp. *Eliza Brewer.* Eliza was the older sister of Noah Brewer, a friend from college. Thankfully, she hadn't seemed to recognize Mia. That would make this exchange ten times more embarrassing.

Mia had done as she was told and had held still as Eliza gently swept Mia's hair from the back of her neck and to the side. Her cool fingers had made Mia shiver as she had tugged the zipper up the last three inches.

"Thanks," Mia had said with relief.

"Of course," Eliza had replied. "I'm—"

"Mia, darling, there you are." Her mother's voice had rung out in the space as she had barged into the room and stepped toward Mia. "What on earth are you doing in here?"

"Mother, hello." She had looked at Eliza, silently asking her to keep her secret. Eliza had nodded once.

"She was helping me out with a wardrobe malfunction." Eliza had held up a button and gestured toward an empty spot on her blouse. Mia could have sworn the button had been there just a moment before. And then, Eliza had winked.

It wasn't until two months later—yesterday on the yacht—that Mia realized Eliza had known it was her the entire time. Or, at least, she'd put it all together since then.

It appeared Eliza Brewer's job in life was to keep saving Mia from embarrassing situations. She'd spent the week after the fundraiser remembering the feel of those fingers on her spine. And grateful that Eliza hadn't told her mother all the secrets she had spilled. But that memory was no longer a secret moment Mia could pull out sometimes when she was lonely. Because she shared that memory with Eliza. Her girlfriend. *Fake* girlfriend.

Mia's stomach pitched as she realized the unfair advantage Eliza had in this situation. Eliza Brewer had a way of sweeping in and fixing things for Mia. And that was the last thing Mia needed. She needed to accomplish something on her own. So, yes, Eliza was objectively attractive. And yes, she made Mia's stomach go all warm inside. But Mia didn't need a girlfriend to save her. Mia didn't need anyone.

Especially not a CEO with the kind of business skills that would put any of her work to shame. She needed to stand out to her parents on her own.

Mia blinked back into the moment and realized the worker was holding the door open with a frown.

"After you." Eliza gestured with one hand to the cable car.

Mia huffed and climbed in the small space, taking the bench seat on the right. Eliza slowly placed one foot on the swinging car, as if testing its soundness, before climbing in and perching on the bench across from Mia. Their knees knocked together and Mia mumbled a half-hearted "sorry" as she struggled to get out of the way.

"Sorry I'm late. Just a second," Eliza said in a tone that revealed nothing. She held up her finger before returning to her phone. She typed rapidly for several seconds before smashing one last key with a flourish. "Thanks, had to get that one sent out."

The morning sun reflected off the windows in the cable car, making Eliza look bright and fuzzy along the edges. Mia sat tentatively on the opposite side. She scowled. "Why did you help me?"

"I'm sorry?" Eliza didn't look up from her phone, scanning over something new.

"At the Fieldings' fundraiser. You zipped me up and then disappeared. I didn't think you knew who I was." There was a hint of accusation in her tone. And Mia wasn't sure why. Eliza had been so kind. But maybe that's what bothered her most. Eliza had a reputation for being brutal. Being honest to a fault. So, why had she treated Mia differently?

"Oh." Eliza's eyes went wide for a moment with realization. "I guess… I mean, I assumed you wanted to be alone."

"With my mom? Yeah, right." Mia was pouting. "I would have gotten the zipper." She needed Eliza to know that she didn't need rescuing. She didn't need *her*.

Eliza sighed and finally shoved her phone in her bag. She crossed her legs, letting her shorts ride up the edge of her thigh, exposing a delicious strip of skin. *Don't get distracted, Mia.* "You just seemed really nervous. Like there was all this—"

she gestured with her hands "—fizzing around inside you. I just wanted to help."

"I guess that makes sense," Mia said, deflated. "I just... I don't like to rely on other people. I need to prove I can do things on my own."

"It was fine. Really. I know you like parties and big scenes and being the center of attention. I was just doing my part to get you back where you belonged."

And there it was. What she'd already known. The world whooshed by underneath them as they steadily climbed the mountain. Eliza wasn't *helping* her. Eliza just saw a party girl when she looked at Mia. Not an equal or a professional. Eliza saw Mia exactly like the rest of the world saw her. Well, that was fine. They didn't need to be friends to get through this week. They just needed to put on a show.

And if that's what Eliza expected, that's what Mia would deliver.

Eliza

Eliza rubbed at her temples again as she kept her eyes on the floor of the cable car and not the ground a hundred feet below. The memory of her phone call with her father this morning was still looming in the back of her mind as she tried to work through Mia's words. He didn't even have the time to knock on her door and sit down with her to talk things over, but he'd called her just as she was about to leave for this ridiculous hike around an active volcano. All to help a woman Eliza wasn't entirely sure liked her.

A woman who didn't even want her help.

A woman Eliza had tried her best to forget about after that stupid fundraiser two months before. Eliza had seen her across the room, biting that damn pencil, and something had unlocked inside her. She thought she'd found a kindred spirit. Someone else who was working just as hard as she was. Maybe someone who had the same pressure. Someone she could relate to.

She hadn't meant to follow Mia into that empty room, but when she'd found her in there, cursing in front of the mirror in a million sequins, she'd been at a loss for words.

"I'm sorry I didn't properly introduce myself that night," she said again. She sighed and set her bag to the side. "But I'm not sorry I helped." She finally lifted her face, just enough to make eye contact with Mia sitting across from her. There was heat in Mia's glare and Eliza felt it everywhere.

"When I took over as CEO, I knew there would be social obligations. And I'm fine in office meetings, or in the boardroom. I can present in front of a hundred people. But dressing up and being social…that's hard for me." God, this was embarrassing. Admitting to Mia she had flaws. Mia would probably end this right now.

But Mia's expression went soft at the edges as Eliza's words fell away. Mia was glamorous and Eliza was never going to really be a part of that world. Even with her auburn hair pulled back into a braid and ridiculous hiking pants that hugged her legs, Mia Knowles was a breathtaking distraction. But a distraction nonetheless. One Eliza couldn't let get in the way of her career.

And definitely not someone she wanted to let down when she inevitably chose her career anyway, just like her father had done to her mother. "I'm not good at making friends."

Mia leaned forward, about to speak, when the cable car hit a transition pole and lurched before clunking back into place. Mia hummed under her breath and leaned back.

Eliza blew out a steady breath. Not that she was afraid of heights. She was fine with tall buildings; it was just the instability of it all. The cable car was so tiny and the hundred-foot plummet below them felt so imminent. And the entire space smelled deliciously like Mia. Like wildflowers and citrus. Like sunshine.

Mia recovered and plastered on a smile, but it didn't reach her eyes. "Lucky for you, Ms. Brewer, I am excellent in front of a crowd. Leave this week to me. Just follow my lead, and I'll have the paparazzi after us in no time." She picked at her nails and recrossed her legs. "That is what you want, right? What you expect? For your family to see you happy and enjoying life?"

Eliza absolutely did not want that. Especially when it posed a risk to Mia. But she *did* want her mom and brother to seeing her dating someone, enjoying the week. And Mia seemed to have decided. She was about to argue with her when the cable car swung backward, her stomach plummeting with it. And then the pulley halted. They'd stopped. They were hovering above a volcano with nothing but rock below and…they'd stopped.

Eliza gritted her teeth and huffed out her nose in an attempt to quell her panic.

"Eliza?" Mia's voice was distant. As if she were underwater. Or maybe Eliza was.

"Did we stop? Why did we stop?" Hesitancy crept into her usually calm voice. The ground was so far away and the cable car was so, so small. And getting smaller by the second. She slammed her eyes shut in an attempt to disassociate. What if it never started again? What if they were stuck forever? What if the cable snapped?

A cool palm pressed gently onto Eliza's knee. "It's okay. You're okay. Someone probably reached the top, and they had to slow us down." Mia's voice was soft. But Eliza's pulse thundered in her ears.

The cable car lurched again and Eliza knew for sure they were falling. Then there came a gentle thud as Mia's body settled next to her.

"Get back on your side!" Eliza screeched. "The weight imbalance. Move back."

Mia shushed her and put her hand on her knee again. "Is this okay?" she asked.

Eliza nodded. And then Mia's thumb moved slowly back and forth. Eliza could hear her exaggerated breathing. "With me, Brewer. Come on. In through her nose, out through her mouth." Mia breathed again and Eliza mimicked it.

After what felt like hours, the cable car lurched once again and Mia's hand was gone as quickly as it had appeared. She maneuvered back to the opposite side and smiled softly at Eliza.

"Sorry, you just seemed really worried."

"Where did you learn to do that?" Eliza asked. It was a technique she'd learned in therapy years ago. The slow breaths, focusing on what she could hear and feel around her.

"Panic attacks," Mia said simply. "I get them sometimes. It used to be worse, but they're not as bad now."

Eliza nodded, amazed at how openly Mia could share something like that. Eliza could barely share how she liked her coffee, let alone details about her mental health. Her father had always taught her she needed to hide her weaknesses, lock them away. Emotions, good or bad, didn't serve anyone in business.

She wanted to tell Mia about her own anxiety, how she worried she wasn't good enough. For her job, for her father, for a girlfriend. How she feared she'd just disappoint someone by choosing her work the same way her father had always done. That's why she was cold. That's why she didn't make friends.

"Mia, I—"

But they'd made it to the top. Whatever bubble they existed in suspended above the mountain was bursting.

Mia cleared her throat and folded her hands into her lap. "Right. You don't have to say anything. Just do your best to pretend you're in love with me and I can take care of the rest."

Before Eliza had a chance to respond, the door slid back on its track and Mia dived out of the cable car, making it swing. Eliza stood slowly and carefully stepped out into the much cooler air. She took a deep breath, grateful she was back on land, but wondering why her head was still spinning.

"Come on, Eliza, everyone is waiting for us." Mia slid her hand into Eliza's and pulled her close. "And they're all watching," she murmured close to her ear. Mia's warm breath traveled along her neck and sent a shiver along the shell of her ear.

Right. Mia promised to put on a show. And damn, she was good at it. She tugged Eliza close, stood on tiptoe and pressed a kiss to Eliza's temple. "Now giggle," she demanded.

Eliza spluttered out a confused laugh that sounded a lot more like a snort.

"I can work with that," Mia mused.

They spent the morning on a guided hike around the craters of Mount Etna. The earth beneath them seemed to tremble with anticipation as they explored, walking over hardened lava juxtaposed with small plants shooting up from the ground in defiance.

Eliza was sure she'd fall at any moment. But Mia was confident and competent, asking the tour guide questions, cracking jokes and doting on Eliza whenever someone was watching. Her fingers would brush the back of her hand, or she'd wink. She even leaned in close, squished their bodies together and took a selfie of them with the island stretching out behind them. Eliza would do anything to get a copy of that photo.

"Told you I could turn it on," she whispered in Eliza's ear. It was such a stark contrast to the Mia from the first dinner. The nervous and awkward Mia that Eliza found so endearing. This was Mia Knowles, exactly as the world expected her to be.

Eliza clasped onto Mia's hand like she was afraid she was going to get lost. She barely said two words. When they'd stopped for water and a rest, Noah sat down next to Eliza on a large rock. The island spread out below them in a stunning tableau.

"You know," he said leaning in close. "This might be the first time I've seen you without your phone clutched in your hands like a lifeline."

Eliza huffed. "Yeah, well, wedding week and all that," she said, trying to hide her annoyance.

"It's a good look for you, that's all I'm saying."

Eliza and her brother had been close once. She was the one who would help him with homework after school, and she turned up music and held dance parties to distract him when their parents were fighting. She had been his person before she moved in with their father and was told it was time to grow up—and time to stop doting on her brother. She'd been so desperate for her father's approval, she'd complied.

Eliza wasn't close to anyone now. This was maybe the longest conversation she'd had with Noah since he was in high school. Guilt tightened around her ribs when she realized that was more than ten years ago.

"You look more like *you*, less like Dad 2.0."

"I'm not Dad 2.0. Don't say that." The words were out of her mouth before she realized what she was saying. The worst part was her brother wasn't wrong. She *was* like their father. Which was why she was supposed to keep people at a distance. She'd just wind up hurting Noah more. She sighed. "I didn't mean... I just..."

"It's fine." Noah stood and nodded toward Cate. "I'm going to check in with Cate. Are you still coming dancing with us later tonight?"

Eliza's feet ached, she felt a headache coming on and her to-do list was a mile long. She couldn't afford to go out dancing tonight. She couldn't really afford any of this. But her brother was talking to her. He *wanted* her there. And the hope in his eyes crumbled all her defenses.

"I'll be there," she said.

"Be where?" Mia asked, walking up behind Eliza and rubbing her shoulders through her jacket. The touch at once calmed her annoyance and sent a new surge of something through her body instead. Something that felt a lot like comfort and desire all wrapped into one.

"Dancing. Somewhere." Eliza made a mental note to check her itinerary when she got back to the room. And then she'd work for a few hours. And then she'd finish work when they got back, no matter what time it was. "I mean, I'm not dancing, but I'm…going. I guess."

"Oh, this is going to be fun," Mia said, a twinkle of something mischievous in her eyes. Eliza felt a low tug in her belly when Mia shimmied her hips. "I'm going to get you on the dance floor, Eliza Brewer. Just you wait."

CHAPTER FIVE

Mia

AT THIS RATE, Mia was never going to get to Cate and Noah's co-ed stag night. She'd been on the phone with her parents for less than five minutes, but each question left her feeling increasingly unsteady. She wanted a bath and a good book, not a night out dancing.

"How is Mount Etna this time of year?" Her mother preferred Europe in the fall after the tourists were gone.

"It was beautiful, Mom. You'd love it." The panoramic view of the cerulean sky as it dipped into the sea and the vast lava deserts weren't the only things that made Mia's breath catch in her throat during the hike. There was also the way the tiny furrow between Eliza's brows would disappear, for just a moment, as if she was just learning how to have fun.

"Mia?" Her father's tone implied that this was

not the first time he'd said her name. "Where are the pictures? I didn't see any posts on social media."

Mia immediately put her dad on speaker and toggled to the photo album on her phone. She had to swipe past three selfies with Eliza before finding something she could *actually* post that would work for her father.

"I was going to add it tonight," she lied. "I need time to make a story out of it."

"Good, good." Her father did not know what she was talking about, thank goodness. "Make sure you use the hashes so people find the resort."

And there it was. She was waiting for her dad to bring this up, and it had taken less than seven minutes. Her dad knew next to nothing about social media and marketing, but he knew Mia was good at getting attention. He hadn't called to check on her, then; he'd called to make sure she was doing her part.

"Of course, Dad." She bit the edge of her thumbnail and stared at the last image from the day: Eliza gripping the edge of the cable car seat as they made their way back down the volcano. She looked very annoyed in the photo, her lips in a thin line as she stared directly into the camera. Mia loved it. And she knew she'd never, ever post it.

"Listen, I have to go," Mia finally stated. "We're going out tonight and I need to meet up with Cate."

"Have fun," her mother said.

Her father added, "Pictures, Mia. Videos. Hashes. Do something helpful."

She said her yeses and I-love-you's and hung up the phone. Cate was her best friend. She wasn't going to use the biggest day of Cate's life to bring notoriety to her family. No matter what her father asked.

It had been a long time, maybe years, since Mia had felt useful in her day-to-day life. But maybe Mia could be of some use to Eliza. Eliza kept sneaking looks at her phone and biting the edge of her lip throughout the day. Mia knew nerves when she saw them. She knew *stress*.

If she was really dating Eliza, she'd stop the nervous habit by biting Eliza's lip and dragging her tongue along the seam until Eliza couldn't remember the time of her next meeting.

But this wasn't real. She knew Eliza was only doing this to convince her brother she wasn't only about work. Mia was a temporary escape for Eliza. And Eliza was doing Mia a massive favor—saving Mia from her lie about a wedding date, or potentially a really sensational scandal that would set back any progress she'd made with her father.

It was better this way. A simple arrangement for the week. She'd see how much she could pull out of Eliza in the time she had. Mia was determined to make that furrow disappear again, if just for a moment.

"Mia? Hello?" Cate waved a hand in front of her face and giggled as Mia blinked back at her. "Wow, you must be thinking about someone else right now."

A knowing smirk crossed her friend's face. Mia's cheeks felt hot. What had she missed?

"What was that?"

"I said, did your dad listen to your idea?" Cate asked as she added another layer of mascara to her lashes. "About the Knowles Foundation? I'm sure he would listen if you just—"

"I don't want to talk about my dad tonight." Mia's chest felt tight as she pushed away the words *Knowles Foundation*. She ignored the memory of her father canceling her request for a meeting. She wasn't sure how to get through to him.

Maybe she should just take out an ad in one of the Brewers' magazines: "Heiress Tells All!" Except it would be about her wanting to do more philanthropy work to expand her family's name. She doubted that would get her father's attention. Maybe he would be happy to know she was making connections with a certain CEO of Brewer Media Enterprises?

She was *not* going to tell her dad about Eliza.

"No, she'd rather talk about Eliza," Beth murmured. She'd been doing this all day. Little side comments about Eliza. If they were designed to frustrate Mia, it was working. But there was a little thrill that she'd somehow managed to get under her ex's skin.

This was the most time Mia and Beth had spent together since before their breakup. Looking at her now, Mia could see the woman she had thought she loved hiding somewhere beneath the scowl. Beth was smart and kind and practical. Above everything else she was practical.

When she'd FaceTimed Mia to break up with her, she'd used data points and given specific, excruciating details of why they weren't a good fit. At the time, Mia had been crushed. But with some time and some distance, Mia knew Beth had been right. Not because of anything Mia could help, but because she and Beth just weren't *right* for each other.

"Beth, stop." Cate narrowed her eyes at her sister. "You promised," she mouthed.

Mia knew she wasn't supposed to see that last part. Maybe Beth didn't like seeing Mia with someone as serious as Eliza Brewer. You didn't get much more serious than the CEO of a multimillion-dollar company who, according to Mia's quick internet search, had never had a serious girlfriend.

By the time they arrived downtown, Mia already felt pleasantly tipsy, just the right amount of fizz running through her. Noah and his groomsmen were already spread out in multiple booths at the back of the club. This place was too small, too intimate, for a separate VIP area like the clubs she visited back home. Mia loved the freedom that came with the tiny island of Sicily. No one seemed to care who she was or what she was doing. She hadn't seen one camera flash in three days.

She spotted Eliza sitting in a booth next to her brother, Noah. Her hair was pulled back for the first time, exposing her neck and creating a delicious curve to the slope of her shoulder. Mia felt the annoying urge to run her fingers along it while they danced. She wondered how far Eliza would take things for the sake of the ruse.

Eliza looked up, catching Mia in a stare, but Mia couldn't make herself look away. "Dance?" she mouthed, tipping her head toward the dance floor. If Eliza said yes, then Mia would enjoy the night. She'd see where things might go.

Eliza shook her head slightly and looked down at her drink. Maybe she was embarrassed.

Or maybe she was in the middle of something. It was fine.

"Mia!" Cate threw both arms up the air, each one holding a shot. "There you are. Hold this." She handed one shot to Mia and then clinked her glass against Mia's.

"To you and Noah!" Mia shouted over the crowd. She was about to take the shot when Cate stopped her.

"To you and Eliza!" she countered. They took the shots and Mia felt the burn all the way down. "Seriously, you two are adorable. She keeps staring at you."

"Really?"

"Oh, wait. Nope." Cate squinted at something behind Mia. "She's back on her phone. And frowning. How do you deal with that? Noah wants to throw the phone into the ocean."

She desperately wanted to turn back and see if it was true. Eliza was in a nightclub. On her phone. Probably with work. Before Mia could intervene, Cate tugged her arm and then they were on the dance floor, surrounded by a sea of moving bodies and music Mia couldn't quite place. One song. And then she'd find Eliza.

But before the song was over, there was someone at her back, a nose bending toward her ear. "You didn't come over to sit with me."

Eliza. She smelled like mint and sugar and

limes. Her breath left a trail of goose bumps on Mia's neck. Mia leaned her head back, but didn't stop moving to the beat.

"You didn't want to dance," she lilted. She moved her hips. Did she just imagine the low growl that came from Eliza's throat?

"You're supposed to be my girlfriend." Eliza put extra emphasis on the word *girlfriend*, as if Mia could miss the annoyance coming off her in waves.

"I guess there's only one option then." Mia turned abruptly, wrapped both hands around Eliza's wrists and tugged her farther into the dance floor. "You'll have to stay and dance with me."

Eliza

When Eliza saw Mia disappear into the sea of dancers, she didn't think. She just stood. Quickly. She tucked her phone into her back pocket as she strode toward the dance floor, as if there was some kind of hook in her stomach she couldn't ignore. The idea of Mia dancing with someone else turned her inside out.

But now Mia was so close, smelling like sweat and citrus and slightly floral. It was driving Eliza wild. She was in so much trouble. Eliza tried to keep her expression neutral, but the steady thump, thump, thump of her pulse under Mia's fingertips no doubt gave her away.

The music shifted into a new song. Mia backed away and whisper-shouted, "It's fine. We don't have to—"

The bass kicked in and everyone shouted, moving in closer all around them. Eliza couldn't resist anymore. She didn't want to. She could let go. For five minutes. What was the worst that could happen?

She reached around Mia's lower back and pulled her close. Her body pressed into Mia's seamlessly. Everything about Mia was easy and smooth. It was the simplest thing in the world to press against the swell of Mia's breasts and look into her eyes.

"I thought you couldn't dance?" Mia asked. Her voice was all breath.

"I said I didn't dance, not that I couldn't dance." Eliza pinched Mia's hip playfully, making her yelp.

"Think you can outlast me on this dance floor?" She smirked.

No. It had been years since Eliza danced with someone. Maybe longer.

"I was made for parties, remember?"

But Mia didn't need to know that Eliza had next to zero game on a dance floor or otherwise.

This was just like the boardroom. Never show your cards. Close the deal.

"Oh, Mia." Eliza leaned down involuntarily, just inches from Mia's mouth. "I can outlast you anywhere."

Mia's eyes darkened, her pupils blown wide. She began moving faster. Her hands were everywhere; her hair was everywhere. Eliza's heart was in her throat and she did her best to keep up. Every time Eliza got a grasp on her, Mia would turn or spin, press her back against Eliza's front. Eliza threw her head back and laughed, lost in the beat, lost in the moment. She just wanted more.

"You know…" Mia threw her arms around Eliza's neck and smiled wickedly. "You don't seem to have convinced your brother."

Eliza immediately turned toward the back corner booth. Mia cupped the side of her face and brought her attention back to Mia.

"Eyes right here, Brewer." Mia's stare was molten hot and Eliza melted beneath it. She was practically jelly in Mia's arms. Mia could make her into anything she wanted. "Cate says you're staring at your phone more than you're staring at me. I think you need to keep up your end of the bargain."

The words were like a splash of cold water. A flush of something close to anger ran down her spine. Her brother, and her mother for that matter, were so quick to judge when she worked. They didn't understand. They *couldn't*. They had no idea the pressure she was under. Not to mention she wasn't sure how to act when she wasn't *on*, when she wasn't *working*.

"Listen, I never said I was going to stop working." Her hands dropped helplessly from Mia's waist. She stopped swinging her hips. She looked down.

"Hey," Mia whispered in her ear. Eliza shouldn't have tried to dance. She shouldn't have tried at all.

"Hey," Mia said again, more fervently. "I've got you. I've got this. Stay here with me. For five minutes. Show them you don't have to be all about work. You can set some of it down with me, Eliza. I can help."

Eliza wanted to believe her. She wanted to believe this was more than a panicked agreement made two nights ago. But she couldn't trust Mia. She barely knew her. Fingers brushed along her shoulder and her entire body shivered in response. She wanted it to happen again.

"Show them," Mia demanded. She raised her brows and leaned in even closer. There was a spray of summer freckles across the bridge of her nose. Another one below her left earlobe. She smelled like sweat, and heat, and everything Eliza Brewer shouldn't want. Everything she couldn't have.

She bumped her nose against Mia's. A question. Mia nuzzled slightly back and shrugged. "Yes," she said. "Why not?"

Eliza didn't want to answer that question. There were a million why-not's, but there was also Mia's perfect pout right at mouth level. She closed the distance between them and brushed her parted mouth over Mia's. It wasn't even a kiss. Their bottom lips barely touched.

It was practically nothing at all.

Still, fireworks went off in Eliza's chest. It was as if the room was simultaneously silent and moving in fast motion all around them. It was ribbons of color, vibrating, pulsing movements, and Mia's mouth quirked into a half smile.

"Do it again," Mia said against her mouth. "Kiss me. It's okay."

Eliza was the one to lean in this time. She took her time running her fingertips along Mia's arm, up her shoulder, into the space at the back of her neck. This was a terrible idea. It would probably end in disaster.

Eliza kissed Mia again.

CHAPTER SIX

Mia

USUALLY AFTER A night out dancing, Mia woke up completely drained. It was too much peopling for her. Too much being *on*. But last night was different. Seeing Eliza let go, just for a moment, made the crowd and the press of bodies completely worth it.

Eliza made it completely worth it.

Mia woke with the sun and ran five miles before she was scheduled to attend the Wednesday-morning brunch. She even scheduled an indulgent massage for later that morning to ease some of her sore muscles.

Cate and Noah's extended families now filled the resort and Mia promised she would be there for the morning brunch on the beach. She'd meant to talk to Eliza about it the night before on the way home from the club, but embarrassingly, she'd fallen asleep as soon as they'd gotten into the car. Eliza had to jostle her awake off her shoulder, coaxing her out of her dream, gently murmuring "Mia" into her hair.

God, Eliza was so *good* at all of this. She really knew how to put on a show. A very convincing show. If Mia closed her eyes, she could still feel the brush of Eliza's tongue on her bottom lip, seeking entrance. If the whole CEO thing didn't pan out, Mia had no doubt she could become an actress.

As Mia approached the private beachside gathering, she searched the tables for Eliza, hoping they'd have a moment to get their stories straight. A long rectangular table with at least twenty place settings sparkled in the morning sun. The crystal goblets of orange juice and water sparkled as the sun broke through the morning clouds. Flowers in oranges, creams and yellows complemented the tablescape with bursts of color in crystal goblets every few place settings.

Mia smoothed out her buttery-yellow sundress and said a silent prayer of thanks that she'd brought more than enough outfits for this wedding. Thankfully, she didn't have to think about the actual wedding day. Her bridesmaid dress had been designed and custom-made months ago.

She spotted Eliza at the far end of the table. Eliza, for her part, was not hiding the wear of the night before. She looked as if she hadn't slept at all. She wore sunglasses and sipped on her coffee. But her phone was suspiciously absent from both her hand and the table. Mia wondered if it had anything to do with their conversation the night before. Before she could figure out exactly where she was supposed to sit, Cate swept her into a hug.

"Good morning, Mia." She leaned in close and smiled conspiratorially at her friend. "I don't know what kind of promise you made her, but she hasn't looked at her phone once this morning." Cate raised a brow and Mia felt her cheeks grow hot.

"I didn't—"

But she had. Hadn't she?

"Whatever it is, keep it up. There's a spot for you next to Eliza. Although I think it's a bit unfair you can't be next to me. Promise we'll catch up later?"

"Of course," Mia said. A pang of guilt hit her stomach. This was her best friend's wedding. And instead of doting on the bride, she was off kissing her fake girlfriend on the dance floor and then falling asleep in her arms. Well, not *in* her arms. Just…on her shoulder.

But she couldn't deny that Eliza seemed calmer this morning. She wore a sleeveless shirt and her hair was pulled up in a simple knot.

Mia sat down next to Eliza and brushed a quick kiss against the edge of her cheek. "Morning," she said softly under her breath. "How did you sleep?"

Eliza stilled for a moment when Mia pulled away. Maybe the brush of lips against her cheek had been too much for morning brunch, but Mia didn't think it was so bad compared to the night before.

"Morning," she murmured. "Sorry, I didn't sleep well."

Eliza sat up and adjusted her place setting. Perhaps she had trouble sleeping because of Mia. Was this fake date arrangement too stressful for Eliza? She already had so much going on.

Mia pushed down her nerves. She could handle a tired Eliza. Hell, Mia often had restless nights when there was a lot on her mind. But last night was blissfully peaceful. She wanted to make everything peaceful for Eliza, too.

A faint buzzing radiated from Mia's small purse. She had it set to do not disturb, so her father must have hacked through the emergency system. It wouldn't be the first time he demanded to be heard. She quickly glanced down at the text message.

Please call me. I know what happened and I'd like to discuss your future plans.

Well, that was weird. A strange thrill rushed through Mia. Had someone told her father about her involvement in the Fielding Foundation? That would be an odd thing for him to text her about out of the blue, but she clung to that hope. Maybe things were starting to go her way after all.

She slipped her phone back into her purse. "That's weird," she said under her breath.

"Now who's on their phone?" Eliza's voice was teasing, but she must have seen something on Mia's face. She leaned in closer. "Is everything okay?"

"What? Yeah, no, everything is fine. It's my father. I'll call him back later." Mia took a small bite of her pastry and let the flaky crust dissolve on her tongue.

"You have just a bit of—" Eliza pointed to her own lip. Mia's cheeks heated as she swiped at the corner of her mouth. "No, wrong side, just…here."

And then Eliza's thumb brushed across the edge of Mia's mouth. The contact sent Mia's stomach plummeting. She was instantly back on that dance floor with Eliza's lips brushing across her own. She composed herself and took a steadying breath. *You're at brunch. With Cate's great-aunt and her grandparents, too. Calm down.*

"Thanks." Mia's words were all breath. Mia wanted to snatch the sunglasses off Eliza's face to get a clear idea of what was running through her head. "You're really good at this."

Eliza cleared her throat and sat up, the moment broken. "I could say the same for you. My brother was beaming this morning. Everyone seems on board with—" she gestured with her coffee cup between them "—this."

As if on cue, Beth dropped into the seat across from them. Her mouth twitched into a not quite frown when she realized who was sitting across from her. Mia had to remind herself, not for the first time, that Beth was the one who broke up with *her*.

"Morning." Mia pushed a chipper tone into her words.

"Mia. Eliza." Beth poured orange juice into a glass and sipped at it. "Did you speak with your father already this morning? He reached out to my parents looking for you, but said he was hoping to speak with you directly."

"I haven't," Mia said. This was weird. Beth and Cate's parents didn't have anything to do with the Fieldings' fundraiser. Unless… A sense of dread pooled in her stomach and her shoulders hunched. A knot of stress was forming somewhere under the surface. "I was going to speak with him after this."

Beth's eyes sparkled with amusement. Mia felt an instant, warm pressure on her thigh. Eliza's hand rubbed gently up and down, grounding Mia in the moment.

"That's smart." Beth set her juice down and glanced between Eliza and Mia. "You know, I have to admit. I was shocked that your parents don't know you're dating Eliza. I figured that they would have met her already."

Mia's heart beat rapidly in her chest. If her parents knew, then someone had told them. It could have easily been anyone here and Mia chastised herself for not thinking this through. If her father found out that she'd gone behind his back and worked with the Fieldings, he would be so angry. Angry for making him look foolish. And angry for stepping out of line.

It was an open secret that the families had a long-standing, unspoken rivalry in the travel industry. When Mrs. Fielding had asked Mia to help out at her annual fundraiser, Mia thought it might have been a joke. But it had turned out to be one of the best experiences of her life. Foolishly, she hoped that by working with the Fieldings she could show her family how silly the rivalry had been.

Nerves coiled tight in her stomach. Of course, word would get back to her father. She placed her hand over Eliza's and squeezed.

"Mia and I were trying to keep things quiet at first. You know, to make sure we could handle the long-distance part of our relationship. It's not easy to be hours apart." Eliza's hand remained warm and steady on Mia's leg. "As you can see, we seem to be doing just fine."

Guilt pooled in Mia's stomach as she peered up at Beth. Her ex stiffened at the words, her eyes going just a bit wide. No one else seemed to notice, but when Beth's eyes flicked up to Mia's for a split second, there was hurt there. And maybe regret?

Mia didn't hold the eye contact. Instead, she watched Eliza's thumb as it slowly traced circles on Mia's thigh. There was a part of Mia, however small that part might be, that wanted Eliza's words to be true. She let herself think, just for a moment, how nice it would be to date someone that had her back. Someone who believed in her dreams and supported her. She reminded herself that Eliza was playing a role. For a temporary week-long facade. No doubt, workaholic Eliza would struggle with a real long-distance relationship. God, she didn't even know where Eliza lived!

Mia's phone pulsed once in her purse. She nudged her purse open and pulled out her phone. And there it was, just below the message from her father. A Google alert for her own name. She didn't want to click on it. She already knew.

The spinning lights of the club last night weren't the only flashes going off around them. Someone must have taken a photo. She closed her eyes and shoved her phone back into her purse. The credibility she'd worked so hard to build the last few months dissolved around her like sand she couldn't catch between her fingers. She was once again just a photo in a magazine.

And her father had seen it. At least he'd be happy. Mia tipped her head from side to side, trying to work out the stress that settled between her shoulder blades and neck whenever the pressure and expectations from her family became too much.

"I need to get out of here," Mia said. Mostly to herself.

"I've got you," Eliza said with a curt nod. "I know just the thing."

Eliza

Eliza didn't know all the hiding places in this resort, but she knew enough to be able to get Mia alone somewhere and figure out what the hell was going on. Eliza was a fixer. A closer. So, whatever this issue was, she was going to make it go away. And then she was going to make whoever upset Mia pay for it.

She was about to push back from her chair when the clink of a spoon against a glass quieted the group. Her father stood, with her mother by his side, and greeted the guests. Eliza's heart squeezed in her chest the same way it always did when she saw her parents side by side. Even though she was a grown adult, watching them stand next to each other as a united front dredged up all those times in her childhood when they hadn't. She knew this was all for show though, and that next week they would go back to not speaking to each other for years, if they could help it.

They'd been happy once. At least, Eliza thought they'd been happy once. And look at them now. Destroyed by time and money and the obligations of work.

"Good morning, everyone. We're so glad you could join us this week to celebrate our son, Noah, as he gets married."

Eliza watched her mother's neutral face as her father spoke. From the outside, you'd never know that she left him because he didn't spend enough time with his family. They'd agreed to co-parent in an efficient manner and in return, she kept up appearances at social engagements and business events. They were the picture-perfect amicably divorced couple.

But Eliza knew the truth. She remembered holidays her dad showed up late to, or not at all. The recitals and school assemblies he'd missed. The way her mother's face would pinch in disappointment when he sent flowers instead of himself. It made her stomach clench into knots.

"As many of you know, my daughter, Eliza, took over as CEO of Brewer Media last year. And while she's been busy learning the business and following in my footsteps, her brother went and fell in love." Eliza's cheeks went hot and she looked down. He always did this. He was a master at belittling and pushing you all at once; backhanded compliments for her brother and careful warnings for her. She gritted her teeth and forced a smile when she realized everyone was looking at her.

Eliza leaned in close to Mia and apologized. "We can go as soon as he's done."

"No," Mia said, plastering on a smile. "It's fine. We should stay. It's nothing. Really."

Anger flared low in Eliza's belly. She knew that face. Mia's smile was thin, flat and didn't reach her eyes. Her shoulders bunched slightly right where the thin yellow straps of her dress clung to her shoulders.

"Mia, you look like you're about to murder

your breakfast roll. So, please, tell me what's going on. You told me last night I could set some of this down. Let me do the same for you."

Something passed over Mia's eyes. Hope, or maybe even more fear. She sighed and closed her eyes, slowly exhaling a breath. "There are photos of us. From the club last night."

The words came out clenched, as if it were painful to say them. Eliza didn't remember photos being taken last night. She just remembered lights and heat and noise. She remembered the salty taste of Mia's neck.

"Are you sure?" Eliza regretted the words as soon as they were out of her mouth. Mia's face flashed with hurt as heat bloomed on her cheeks. She nodded once.

"I have alerts on my phone. And apparently… so does my dad. Or at least, I think he does. He keeps messaging me."

The words sank in and Eliza's stomach pitched. If there were photos of them, then this wasn't some fake dating thing for a week at a secluded wedding they could quietly let go. If there were photos of them, then the world knew. Her mind went back to last night. The flashes. As they kissed. It wasn't just the lights. Someone was in there. And Mia didn't want to be seen.

"I'll fix this," Eliza says.

"There's nothing to fix. It's already done.

And it's not like you leaked the photos. It's not like you could know how something like that would set me back years in a plan with my dad."

Eliza knew that feeling better than Mia could imagine. Her dad insisted she keep her image perfect, never showing a hint of weakness. He'd be so annoyed to see pictures of her out dancing when she was supposed to be working. Eliza was supposed to be the responsible one. Not the one who was out partying. She had clients to impress. Eliza needed to see these photos. And she needed to solve this. Maybe she knew someone and could get them to take it down.

Mia squeezed her hand. "Eliza, it's fine. This kind of stuff happens all the time. I'll be okay. I'll think of something." She was trying to be brave. Eliza wanted to reach out and tuck the strand of hair behind her ears.

She raised her fingers to do it, fake dating scheme be damned, when everyone around her raised their glass and said in unison, "To Cate and Noah." She fumbled for her own glass of champagne that had appeared in the last few minutes and clinked it against Mia's before taking a tiny sip.

Mia sighed and pulled her phone from her bag. "Look. It's not that bad."

Eliza took the phone, unable to tell Mia that she couldn't care less about how she looked in the photo. All she cared about was Mia. But still, she searched for her name. And there, above her family's company website and the article from *Forbes 40 under 40* from last spring was the link to the photo.

Eliza clicked on it without hesitation. And there, front and center, was a photograph of Mia and Eliza in the club. Eliza knew that exact moment. It was just before she sealed her lips on Mia's for a second time. Their bodies were pressed close and Mia was leaning toward her.

God, Mia looked gorgeous. The bright lights made her skin glow and her mouth was curved into a curious smirk. Eliza's hand rested on Mia's lower back and there was no denying the connection between the two of them. Mia was very good at putting on a show. She even had Eliza convinced for a minute.

Eliza was about to click out of the photo. She didn't want to get caught. She didn't want Mia to know how looking at that picture made her feel. But just before she closed the app, the photo credit caught her eye. And the company running the photograph.

It was a subsidiary of Brewer Media. Someone had taken Eliza's photo. Someone had submitted the photo. And someone had approved this photo. And Eliza Brewer was not the one who approved it.

"Come on," Eliza said, standing and dropping her napkin into her chair. "Let's get out of here."

Mia didn't question her. She just rose and silently put her hand in Eliza's, turning her back to Beth, who was now giving them some top-notch side-eye. If Eliza didn't leave right now, she was going to do something she regretted. She was so grateful that Mia trusted her. She pulled her close and they darted away from the beach as Cate and Noah kissed to thunderous applause.

CHAPTER SEVEN

Mia

ELIZA PULLED MIA down a walk and through the private courtyard at the edge of the property. At this rate they were going to wind up lost. Or in the middle of an olive orchard.

"Eliza, slow down."

Thankfully, Eliza listened. She took a sharp turn and ducked into one of the buildings. "Come back to my room with me."

"Excuse me?"

"That's not what I… I just. Can we talk somewhere private?"

Mia's heart thundered in her chest. This was when Eliza was going to end things. End this charade. She was going to tell her it was too much to be associated with a party girl. Mia knew she deserved this. She had been reckless last night. She never should have danced with Eliza in a club, in the middle of town, let alone kissed her. Twice. And then lingered, her fingers toying with Eliza's chain at the back of her neck.

That had been stupid.

"I don't know if that's a good idea," Mia admitted. Her voice was loud and reverberated off the marble floors of the hallway. This part of the resort looked familiar. She remembered the tile, the floor-to-ceiling windows on one side and the cavernous entrance to the resort's spa.

The spa. Her appointment was in ten minutes. In the turmoil of the message from her father, she'd forgotten all about it. The woman at the desk looked up and a broad smile spread across her face.

"Miss Mia," she said in a warm tone. "Welcome back, Miss Mia."

Eliza gave Mia a confused look. But Mia knew this team. She'd been here before the opening. And she'd visited the spa more than once. The sauna was great after her morning run. Not to mention the massage on her calves. She waved and offered a hello in her best stilted Italian.

"Your neck. Your shoulders." The woman pointed at her. "You're so tense. Too much running."

"Oh, no." Mia forced her shoulders to relax, even as she felt the slight pinch. These stressful situations always manifested in her shoulders. Mia didn't have the heart to tell her it had nothing to do with running. "I'm fine. Can I reschedule my appointment? Something has come up."

But the woman wouldn't have any of it. "We have time now. You and your *amore*. We have time. Come. Relax."

Mia desperately wanted some time. She needed Eliza to slow down and think things through. To change her mind about stopping this arrangement with Mia. She grabbed Eliza's hand and pleaded with her eyes.

"You said you wanted to go somewhere private," Mia murmured. "No one will find you here."

Eliza bit the edge of her lip. Mia thought for sure she would turn her down. But then Eliza slid a hand to one of Mia's shoulders and pressed at the knot forming under the surface. God, it hurt and felt wonderful at the same time. Just like everything else with Eliza Brewer.

"You do seem tense. I didn't mean to be selfish. Let's get you a massage. Then we can talk."

Mia breathed a sigh of relief. Eliza's hand trailed from her shoulder down her arm and down to her wrist. She tangled their fingers together and Mia pulled her into the spa.

They were led to a dimly lit room with music playing low. There was a fountain of water babbling in the corner and two white fluffy robes resting on one wide massage table bed.

"Okay, so this must be your room," Eliza said. "I can go wait outside until mine is ready. Or until you're done."

"No," the woman said. "It's no trouble. I moved this to a special couple's massage. You are a couple, yes? So, Mia, you will lay down first, and I will show your *amore* how to release some of the tension in your neck and back. And then you will do the same for her."

Mia knew what a massage entailed. And she'd even done a couples massage in the past. But then, there were had been two beds. And she and her girlfriend had lain side by side while they were given massages at the same time. She'd never had someone else who wasn't a masseuse touch her before. Massage her before.

"Oh, I'm sorry. Maybe there has been a miscommunication. Eliza doesn't... I mean, she doesn't need to—"

"No, it's fine." Eliza's eyes went focused and determined. The way Mia assumed she must look in the boardroom. "I can do this. I'm, um, happy to learn."

"Then I will leave you two to change. Miss Eliza? You can put on a robe for now. Mia, go ahead and lay down on the bed. I will be right back."

As soon as the door closed a giggle bubbled up from Mia's lips. "Eliza. I swear. I didn't know."

"How can you be laughing right now?" Eliza hissed.

"You don't have to do this. We can fake one of us being sick." Mia shrugged and felt the pull in her shoulder.

"No, you're in pain. We can stay. I'll turn around while you get on the bed."

Mia nodded. She wasn't uncomfortable with her body, but she wasn't going to push Eliza. So, as soon as she turned, Mia removed her sundress and her bra and set them both on a chair before lying face down.

"Okay," she said. She closed her eyes and let her body melt into the massage table. "My eyes are closed."

Eliza didn't respond. In the silence, Mia heard a zipper slowly work its way down tine by tine before soft fabric fell onto the floor. She squeezed her eyes shut and tried not to think about Eliza stepping out of her pants. Then there was a soft rustle and an exhale. The camisole. And finally, two quick flicks of some kind of clasp. Mia didn't imagine what kind of bra Eliza wore. She tried to keep her mind blank, until Eliza let out a soft hiss, no doubt as her body felt the cool air hit her now-naked skin.

Mia steadied her breath. "Okay over there?"

"Yeah." Eliza's voice came out all breath. The rustle of cotton and the undeniable sound of Eliza tying the robe around her generous hips filled the room. "Just cold. I'm...decent."

Mia smiled into the bed, but didn't lift her head. God, Eliza was a surprise at every turn. Mia knew this took courage and she didn't want to spook her.

"You don't have to touch me. I promise. I know this is weird. But thank you for doing this."

"Of course, that's what fake girlfriends are for."

At that reminder Mia felt a small clench in her chest. Eliza wasn't calling this off. *Yet.* If they could get through the world's most awkward massage, then maybe they could get through the rest of the week still intact. Mia felt a rush of embarrassment at what was about to happen. Maybe she could convince her masseuse to just demonstrate and not make Eliza Brewer touch her.

"All set in there?" The woman's voice cut through the silence of the room.

"Yes," Eliza said smoothly. As if this wasn't about to happen.

Eliza

When Eliza woke up this morning, there wasn't a world in which she imagined she would have her hands on Mia's shoulders, gently rubbing her thumb into the crease of her neck in order to relieve some tension. And yet, here she was, adding one more moment with Mia to the bank of things she'd have to look back on when this week was over and the charade was done.

She pressed her thumb over the knot and Mia let out a small moan of relief. Eliza lost her goddamn mind.

The masseuse gave her some more pointers and showed her how to access the warmed oil and then left Eliza alone in this room with Mia laid out naked and exposed on the table, only a thin sheet covering her from the waist down and absolutely nothing covering the top.

"You can stop now," Mia huffed out. "I'm so sorry. This is so awkward."

"Don't be silly. You have so much tension." Yep, that was why Eliza couldn't keep her hands off Mia. It was for her physical health. She pressed down on the tendon at Mia's neck and Mia let out another moan that seemed on the edge of pain. "Are you okay?" Eliza's fingers froze in place.

"Yeah. Sorry. It's just stress. I carry it all in my shoulders."

"What are you stressed about?" Eliza asked. She pressed again, more gently this time. Maybe if they talked then they could ignore the fact that neither of them was wearing clothes. "Is it this? Us?"

"No," Mia said quickly. "Yes?" She didn't speak for a moment and Eliza took the opportunity to run her thumbs into the scapula of Mia's shoulders. Mia was like a cat. The more Eliza touched her, the more she relaxed, and the more she talked. Eliza repeated the movement.

"Yes?"

"It's my father. I thought you and I could help each other this week. I didn't want to tell Cate that my date had fallen through. I mean, how pathetic is it that I couldn't get someone to come with me to Sicily for my best friend's wedding?"

"I don't think it's pathetic. I mean, I'm here alone." At least, she had been alone. Now she was definitely something else.

"My parents tried to set me up with someone. It was a disaster. My dad is very concerned about my image. My family's image."

"So, when he saw that picture of us, he got mad." Eliza should have known. The photo wasn't necessarily scandalous, but she wasn't exactly thrilled to be in the news. In the news of a magazine owned by her company. As soon as her phone was back on, she was going to find out who did this. And someone was going to get fired.

Mia snorted. "Worse. I think he's proud. I don't know. Maybe? He's either mad or really impressed. I'm guessing he just wants more photos." Eliza felt Mia slump into the bed. "The only thing he wants from me is to be in the media. He doesn't actually care about my work. He doesn't care about my passions. Just the tabloids."

Eliza thought back to the first time they met, at the Fieldings' fundraiser. Mia had been so worried about her parents. Eliza had no idea she was under this kind of pressure.

"Mia, I'm sorry. I didn't know." Eliza blew out a breath. Mia was being honest with her. Eliza yearned to confide in Mia, but her father's voice echoed in her thoughts, warning her against vulnerability. Reminding her she couldn't trust anyone.

Eliza couldn't be honest with Mia. She could barely be honest with herself. Swallowing hard, she closed her eyes and spoke in a soft voice. "My father doesn't want me to date at all. He spent his whole life building this company, turning it into something our family can be proud of. Something he could pass down to me. Even when I was younger, he never saw Noah as an option. I've always been the dependable one. And I can't get distracted. I have to stay focused. To make him proud."

"Is this arrangement causing stress for you? Do you need to be working right now? We can—" Mia began sitting up on her elbows, ready to leave the bed. Eliza knew in about two seconds she was going to see more of Mia Knowles than she thought she'd be able to handle. The edge of her breasts and the dip of her rib cage were already in sight. Everything inside Eliza coiled tight, centering low in her belly.

Nope. No.

Eliza pressed her back down and looked away.

"No. It's fine," Eliza said as softly as she could. Mia tipped her head and stared at Eliza, concern and worry in her brow. "Hey. Hey? It's okay. It's going to be okay."

Eliza wasn't sure what she was promising. But she hated seeing Mia like this.

Mia's voice came out low and soft. Timid. "I know you're a private person. But I promise I didn't do this on purpose. And I understand. If you want to end things."

Eliza's heart thudded in her chest. In just a few days, Eliza would go back to New York and this would all be a memory.

She didn't have much time at all.

She searched for what little truth she could give Mia. "I don't *want* to end things." And she didn't, she realized. But she would. She pressed her fingertips down Mia's spine, counting the notches as she went. "We still have two more days. We will get through the wedding. And then we can work out some kind of breakup in a few weeks. Something amicable. Maybe we can just blame the distance."

Mia huffed out a breath into the mattress. "Please, whatever we do, can we *not* blame the distance? It's the reason Beth and I... The reason she—"

"No problem. We can think of something else."

Mia sat up on the bed, wrapping the sheet around her. Eliza reached out without thinking and tugged it up to keep it secure. Mia's breath caught in her throat, filling the quiet space around them.

Eliza had been touching Mia for the last twenty minutes, but the brush of her fingers, through a sheet, had done something else to her entirely. And Eliza knew Mia was affected just as much as she was. She could see the evidence of it as Mia's nipples pebbled beneath the thin sheet.

"You know—" Mia's words were low and dreamy, or maybe that was just Eliza's wishful thinking. "In another lifetime, I think we could have made each other really happy."

It was all just too much. Eliza wanted badly to believe her. Mia already made her happy and she didn't want to burst whatever bubble of happiness they had right now. Eliza didn't think.

She just took half a step closer, her mouth mere inches from Mia's soft, pink pout.

"Could you imagine?" Mia murmured. Her eyes were hooded and she kept staring at Eliza's mouth. "An aimless heiress and a CEO? This would never work. Not in this life. I can't believe no one has figured out we're not in love."

"Right," Eliza whispered. She bit the edge of her lip and watched as Mia's eyes dropped there again. Was she thinking about their kiss last night, too? Desire pooled low in Eliza's belly as she realized how close she'd moved to Mia, naked beneath the thin sheet. Her words were all breath. A half plea for Mia to stop her if she didn't want this. "Definitely not in love."

Two soft raps on the door caused Eliza to freeze, her mouth hovering just over Mia's. She cleared her throat and pulled back.

That had been close.

Eliza was suddenly grateful the spa woman returned, instructing them to switch places. She was able to bury her face into the soft sheets and didn't have to continue the conversation that had been interrupted. But when the two women left the spa, she was certain something had shifted. Something she didn't want to admit to.

CHAPTER EIGHT

Mia

MIA STARED AT her phone and willed herself not to read the comments. She had half a mind to turn off her Google alerts, too. She'd tried to call her dad back after the massage, but the call went straight to voicemail. He was either very happy or very upset.

Mia had been a mess this morning. Frazzled and frustrated and coming undone. And Eliza had been right there. Calm and collected. Her phone was nowhere in sight. She'd even dared to put her hands on Mia and press at the knot of tension in her shoulders, working away steadily until it was no more than a sore tender spot.

When it had come time for Mia to return the favor, she had to close her eyes as she rubbed in gentle circles down Eliza's shoulders and then back. Eliza was so lovely, sprawled out on the massage table. Her skin was soft and smooth and pliant under Mia's touch. At one point, Eliza had let out an accidental moan that made Mia lose focus for a moment.

Mia had meant to tell her thank you when they were done, but Eliza had to run off for a meeting. She hurriedly told Mia she'd see her tonight at the sunset beach mixer.

Mia spent the afternoon wandering the property. She stepped into the olive orchard next door and rambled among the trees. There was so much beauty in the trees, the fields. It renewed her spirit to be so close to nature. When Mia was younger, she'd run through the orchards and scrape her knees and dream of her future. But her mother has chastised her and her father reminded her that it was improper for an heiress to run amok. So now she stuck to treadmills and marathons, and running when she could be photographed and handed a medal.

Mia stretched her limbs in the warm sun and contemplated her future. There was what her father wanted…but what did Mia want? Did she want to be constantly under his thumb? She kept letting him win, even at the expense of her own happiness.

Eliza didn't seem to enjoy the pressure from her father, but she appeared to thrive as CEO. She was confident and charismatic and calm under pressure. She was at her best when her fingers were flying on her keyboard.

But that wasn't Mia.

By the time she'd made it back to her room and showered for the mixer, it was too late to call her parents again. But she was going to tell them. As soon as she got home. She was done with these games. She wanted to pursue a career in philanthropy—with or without her family's support. She'd find a nonprofit to work for. She'd open her own nonprofit. She'd figure it out. Worst-case scenario, she'd wait until she was thirty, and then use her trust fund to do it.

With a start Mia realized the only person she really wanted to tell about this revelation was Eliza. She imagined Eliza's smile when she told her. It sent a thrill down Mia's spine. *Thank you for giving me a massage. Also, I think your fingers are magic because they helped me realize I don't need my dad's approval. And also, will you please let me maybe put those fingers in my mouth?* God, that was unhinged.

But Eliza made Mia a little unhinged.

She sighed and adjusted her cotton dress before heading out of the hotel room. A casual mixer on the beach was much needed after the luxurious brunch this morning and an afternoon in the sun.

When she arrived, Mia realized she'd severely

underestimated what a beach mixer for Cate and Noah's wedding would entail. She'd dressed more casually than she should have. Everyone else seemed ready for a fancy dinner, not a beach party. Embarrassment flushed hot in her cheeks. This was exactly the kind of thing her parents would chastise her for. But she was twenty-six, not sixteen. So she decided to fake confidence in her pink shimmery beach cover-up dress and strode over to Cate.

"Mia, you made it!" Her best friend's voice carried through the crowd.

Cate stood near one of the bars, Noah on one side and Beth on the other. Noah wore a dark suit with the sleeves rolled up and Cate was in a floral cocktail dress. Even Beth was in a short black dress. But they were all barefoot. The one part of this evening Mia seemed to get right.

Mia hugged Cate, then Noah, and finally gave Beth an awkward nod. "I definitely did not get the black-tie beach mixer memo," Mia sighed. "I'm going to go change."

"It's fine." Cate waved her hand around, the bright orange-and-red cocktail swirling in the glass. "No one is going to notice."

It wasn't the comfort her friend thought it was. Mia felt even more out of place. She took one step backward, determined to slip into something better suited for the occasion, and bumped into someone. Warm arms encircled her waist and a familiar scent enveloped her as Eliza held her tight. Eliza nuzzled her face into Mia's neck and said in a low voice, but still loud enough for everyone else to hear, "Don't you dare change out of this dress."

She squeezed Mia's hip. The press of her fingers was a reminder of that morning. Her breath on Mia's neck was a memory of the kiss they'd almost shared in the dark, close-quartered spa treatment room.

Mia sucked in a breath of shock and surprise.

"I like you like this," Eliza said again. She let go and backed up to take in Mia's soft summer dress.

Mia felt goose bumps rise along everywhere Eliza's eyes trailed. My God. They had one fake kiss and one almost kiss and Mia's body couldn't contain itself. She worked to keep her composure, but she knew her entire body was flushed.

Eliza wore a fitted suit similar to her brother's. But Eliza had left the jacket open and the top few buttons of her blouse were undone. Mia's gaze dropped to Eliza's deliciously soft stomach and up to the thin line of cleavage peeking out from her blouse. It was the least put together Mia had ever seen Eliza in public. And she liked it. A lot. Mia tugged at the collar of her blouse.

"Speak for yourself," she murmured. "This looks great."

"Um, okay you two. Can you try to keep it together for at least a few hours?" Cate teased with a lilt and a knowing smile.

Beth snorted and rolled her eyes. Mia wanted to say something, but couldn't be bothered. Instead, she turned to Eliza and winked. "No promises," she giggled. Then she looped her hand in Eliza's and pulled her from the group. "We'll catch up with you all later."

Mia needed to get Eliza alone for a few minutes. She wanted to tell her thank you. And she wanted to tell her about her plan. She was going to stand up to her father. And she was hoping that maybe Eliza would be willing to keep the fake dating thing going. Just for another week or so, until after she talked to her parents. Otherwise, they would blame this declaration on the breakup and wouldn't take her seriously at all. And Mia needed them to take this seriously.

"Thanks for covering for me back there," she said, leaning in toward Eliza. She found a cabana a few rows down with loungers facing the ocean. The butter-yellow-striped canvas gave the feeling of privacy.

"Oh." Eliza seemed to take a minute to realize what Mia was referring to. She shrugged. "It's a good dress."

"It's pink and shimmers in the light. Everyone else is in black and white."

Eliza shrugged again, a small smile tugging at the corners. "It's blush. Barely pink. And you look good."

"You think I look good?" Mia smiled and batted her lashes at Eliza.

"Stop. You know you're gorgeous."

Mia felt heat spread across her body and low in her belly. Something in Eliza's eyes told Mia this wasn't just an act. There was a part of Eliza, however small that part might be, that wanted Mia. Mia was tempted to see how far she could push Eliza. How far she could push herself. What would Eliza do when there was no one there to see?

"Whatever," Mia said instead. "I wanted to talk to you. About this morning." Mia was going to tell her all the ways Eliza was wonderful. How much she'd helped. How giving she'd been. It was all on the tip of her tongue.

"It was nothing," Eliza said, brushing the comment aside. "There isn't anything to thank me for. We both knew this week was going to put us in some weird situations."

"Weird?"

"Yeah. You know. Awkward." Eliza raised a

brow and mimed massaging. "But I think we convinced the masseuse. That was close."

"Yeah," Mia said softly. Well, someone had been convinced—Mia. God, what a fool she was. Mia swallowed thickly and looked away. Whatever opening she'd thought she'd had with Eliza just a few moments before was gone. Eliza was back to treating this, treating her, like a business deal.

"What did you want to talk about?" Eliza asked. She sat on the edge of a chaise and crossed one leg at the ankle. Grains of sand clung to the bottom of her feet like sugar. Eliza absently brushed them away.

Her business-deal face was on, like she was already closed off.

"Oh, nothing. Just something about my parents." Mia waved it away. She didn't need to trouble Eliza with that nonsense. How could she explain it? Compared to Eliza's father, Mia's troubles with her parents seemed trivial.

"Your parents are here," Eliza said with alarm.

"No. They're not here. They couldn't come. It's just—"

"Are you sure?" Eliza looked beyond Mia.

Mia turned and sure enough, her parents were less than fifty feet away talking with another couple. Her parents. Who were supposed to be in New York. Her parents who told her they couldn't come to this event, but they trusted her to handle everything.

Her parents were here. They didn't trust her at all.

Eliza

Mia's face went from confused to upset and then to schooled, perfect calm in a matter of seconds. Eliza wasn't sure what Mr. and Mrs. Knowles were doing at the mixer, but it was very clear that Mia was not expecting them. And Mia didn't seem to be the kind of person who liked surprises.

That must be why Eliza felt the urge to reach out and put a calming hand on Mia's shoulder. To pull her close and whisper in her ear that she could rely on Eliza. That she wasn't going anywhere. But she didn't want to make a promise she couldn't keep.

"Umm, how do you want to handle this?" Eliza said quickly. They hadn't discussed Mia's parents. At all. Were they in on the fake dating arrangement? Was Eliza supposed to keep the act going, or turn things down a bit? She felt like she was about to give a presentation and had left her laptop and notes back in her office.

"Mom? Dad?" Mia waved at her parents from a distance, catching their attention.

Her dad looked from Mia to Eliza and frowned. Okay, so maybe this was going to be even worse than Eliza had thought. She had no experience with impressing a partner's parents. She barely had experience with her own parents. Once her parents divorced, she spent more time caring for Noah and making sure he was okay than either of their parents. And once she was a teenager, she moved in with her father and he treated her more like an intern than his daughter.

She didn't know what to say or how to act. Panic coursed through her as the two people approached. Her own parents had kept their distance from her and Mia, watching her with distrustful amusement and frustration. But Mia's parents marched over with shock and concern. Eliza needed to prove she was trustworthy.

"Hello. I'm Eliza Brewer, CEO of Brewer Media. It's so nice to meet you. I'm sorry we didn't tell you we were dating. It's so nice to meet you. I already said that." Eliza clamped her lips shut and thrust her hand out, practically wiggling her fingers waiting for a handshake. "Your daughter is an amazing person."

Mr. and Mrs. Knowles stared at Eliza with amusement. Finally, Mrs. Knowles leaned in and offered Eliza a stiff hug. Mr. Knowles took her hand and shook it.

"Of course, we knew you were dating," he said with a barrel laugh.

The hair went up on Eliza's neck. She knew when someone was lying—and this man had no idea who she was. "Mia told us all about it. Our daughter wouldn't keep something so important from us just to have it come up in the magazines first."

Mr. Knowles had a high forhead, a clean jawline and perfectly manicured fingers that he placed on Mia's shoulder before giving a slight squeeze. Her shoulders pinched up just slightly and Eliza wondered how much of Mia's stress and tension came from years of hunching just like that.

"Of course," Eliza said. "Well, it's nice to meet you. Officially. In this capacity."

Mia's eyes flitted to Eliza's and held her gaze. They seemed to be saying *thank you* and *I'm sorry* and *what a mess* all at once. Eliza tried to push all the sentiments back in her responding smile. *I've got you. You aren't alone. Let me carry some of this.*

Mia's parents settled onto the loungers and Eliza had a growing fear that she was about to be interrogated. Or maybe like she was back in boarding school and a lecture from the dean was imminent.

"Can I grab the two of you a drink?" The

words tumbled from her mouth as she rushed to stand.

"Isn't there a server who will do that?" Mrs. Knowles asked as she looked around the space.

"I'm happy to do it," Eliza said. "How about the signature cocktail?"

When Mia's parents finally agreed, Eliza couldn't get away fast enough. She would just give them a few minutes to gather their thoughts. Then she would come back, give them their drinks and Eliza would spend the rest of the night trying to get the Knowleses to like her.

When Eliza approached the bar, her brother and Cate were gone. But another familiar face was leaning on the counter, surveying the scene like a lion looking out over his pride.

"Father," Eliza said in a formal tone. "Nice to see you at one of these prewedding events."

"Oh, don't be like that. I'm here, aren't I? And I'm technically *retired*. The better question is, what are *you* doing here?"

Eliza stiffened at her father's brusque tone. She was used to him putting unspoken pressure on her, but no worse than she put on herself. Eliza shrugged.

"I turned my phone off for the day. I put up an out-of-office notification. It should be fine."

"I am well aware you have an out-of-office

response on, Eliza. I've received it three times today."

Bile rose up in the back of her throat. What was her dad doing? He was supposed to be retired. Not sending his daughter work emails from his son's wedding. Still, she couldn't ignore the panic rising in her throat.

"Is something wrong?"

Her father frowned at her. She would have preferred a sneer. This just looked like inevitable disappointment. "Apparently nothing I couldn't take care of." He took a long sip of a warm brown liquid in his glass. "Turn on your damn phone, Eliza."

And then he walked away. Eliza felt like she was five years old. Or she was twenty-five, receiving her preplanned promotion to vice president of the company. She felt like she was seventeen, being told what to major in and where to go to college. She felt like she was fifteen, breaking up with her high school girlfriend because it wasn't part of her father's ten-year plan.

Eliza held her breath, reached into her coat pocket and pulled out her phone. She hated that she was so predictable. He probably knew she still had it on her, even if it was tucked away.

Her phone immediately began buzzing with missed calls, voicemails, text messages and emails. She focused in on her work inbox and made quick work of identifying anything that involved her father.

A few story proofs, a meeting scheduled for next week and there, toward the bottom of the pile, was an email with an attachment. The subject line read Sensitive photos. It was an email from one of their photographers. One of the ones paid to be at this wedding. With six versions of the photo Eliza now knew all too well. Eliza and Mia dancing, Eliza and Mia kissing, Eliza and Mia with their bodies pressed close.

The details of the email blurred together as Eliza tried to make sense of it.

Hey boss, I don't think you want these public, but I couldn't resist snapping a photo of you and your partner at the club. Let me know if need anything else.

Her father wasn't even on the original email. Which meant he must still be monitoring her work email with his old account. Anger burned up in her fast and red-hot.

These photos are great. Please add one to the celebrity column for tomorrow. If Eliza has time to party, we may as well get some sales out of it.

Her father. Her father had approved the photo. Eliza couldn't care less about the photograph. They regularly included photos of their family at events, especially when they were with other people society cared more about. And Mia Knowles was definitely someone people cared about.

But he hadn't asked her. And this time she would have said no. She knew Mia was weird about paparazzi. She knew Mia didn't want to be in the spotlight.

The messages went back and forth for a bit. Her father finally stated he spoke to Eliza and she gave her approval. A fist clenched around her heart and squeezed tight. He'd lied to the editor. He'd lied to her. He didn't trust her. Or respect her.

But above all, her heart hurt for Mia. She had to tell her that the photograph came from her company. That she was the reason it went to print. It made Eliza's chest ache.

"Can you put your phone away for five minutes?"

Her mother's voice was a hiss in her ear. Eliza immediately pocketed the phone and sighed. She and her mother weren't close. When her parents had split, Eliza chose to live with her father. Noah split time between the two. Her mother viewed it as a betrayal, but Eliza just saw it as a practicality. She had a lot to learn and she wasn't going to learn it from California, where her mother had moved after the divorce.

"Hello, Mother." Eliza decided to play nice. She was already mad at her father. No need to add more to the mix. "You're right. It's away. Are you having fun?"

Her mom stared at her for a moment, no doubt stunned by the lack of pushback.

"Maybe that Mia girl is good for you," she finally said, taking another sip of her drink. "Where is she? I wanted to introduce myself."

Eliza turned to look back at the cabana. *Crap*. The drinks. "She's sitting with her parents. I'm supposed to be getting drinks."

"Her parents? Wow, this is serious."

Eliza shrugged. She didn't want to lie any more than she already was.

"Yeah, I guess it is."

"Well, you seem happy. Don't let go of it. Your father and I were happy once. And then we ruined it with animosity and work and not being honest with each other. Your brother seems to have found his match in Cate. Maybe you've found yours, too."

Eliza swallowed back a response. She couldn't explain to her mother, of all people, that the only reason she seemed happy was because work couldn't ruin a fake relationship.

The bartender handed Eliza four drinks and

her mother eyed her curiously. "Don't let your father determine what happiness and success looks like for you. His dreams don't have to be yours. And his pressure has no place on your back."

Eliza was used to this kind of speech from her mother, but she wasn't used to it stinging quite so much. She'd usually have a quick comeback like *I like my work* or *I also don't need to define myself by your criteria.* Or even *If I didn't take this on, then it would be Noah. And we both know he'd be miserable.*

Her mother always seemed to forget that Noah's choices and her own choices left Eliza with no choices at all. She took on the responsibilities of the family, the company, so they wouldn't have to. And she'd do it again.

But she didn't want Mia to wind up like her mother. Resenting Eliza and spending the rest of her life regretting the years they spent together. No, not Mia. Anyone. Eliza didn't mean Mia. They weren't dating. So there was no possibility Mia would end up like this.

They just needed to stick to the plan. But first Eliza needed to deliver these drinks. And make it through one more night without kissing Mia Knowles.

CHAPTER NINE

Mia

THIS WAS A bad idea. It was after midnight and she shouldn't be a baby about all this. But she couldn't stay in that suite one more minute. Not after her parents' constant barrage of questions. But now she was in her slippers and had the bathrobe from the bathroom closet draped over her shoulders, which felt a lot like the one Eliza had worn in the spa earlier that day.

She knocked again. "Please be awake, please be awake," she murmured under her breath. She was about to knock a third time when the door cracked open two inches and Eliza's face popped into view.

"Mia?" She blinked a few times, as if she couldn't be sure this was actually Mia standing in front of her. Mia flushed as Eliza's eyes took in her thin cotton pajamas, exposing more than Mia would like. "You're…you're in pajamas."

out moving an inch and smiled. "We will both sleep in the bed. We're adults. And I don't think either of us are going to win this fight. Maybe this way we can both get some sleep."

"You aren't sleeping either?"

"I never sleep well," Eliza said. "Even if I can fall asleep, I'm usually up after just a few hours, my brain in overdrive."

Mia hmmed to herself and considered Eliza's words. Mia may have stress in her neck, but Eliza's entire life was ruled by it. She wished she could relieve some of Eliza's burden the way Eliza had done for her.

She followed quietly as Eliza led her to the bedroom, pointing out the bathroom, the extra pillows and the toothbrush from the toiletries kit. When Mia finally collapsed onto her side of the massive bed, she sank into the pillows and sighed contentedly.

"Your bed is so much better than mine," she pouted when Eliza joined her on the other side, at least two feet of space between them.

"The beds are exactly the same, I'm sure." Eliza's lips twitched. Mia knew she could get punchy and ridiculous when she was tired. It was better to stop talking now. "Go to sleep."

Mia tried to close her eyes, but her body was all too aware of the warm heat coming from the other side of the bed. She tried her best to keep still, but the nervous energy made her twitch and clear her throat and then sigh.

"Mia?" Eliza's voice reverberated in the darkness.

"Yes?"

"Is something wrong?"

"No. Yes. It's just… I can't get comfortable. I have too much running through my mind and I—"

Mia felt a tug on her arm, and then Eliza was pulling her close, into the crook of her arm. "Is this okay?"

"What are you doing?"

"I don't know," she answered. "When I was really little and I couldn't sleep, my mom would run her fingers through my hair, rub at my scalp. Like this." She trailed her fingers through Mia's curls, giving gentle pressure with each pass. "Is this helping?"

Mia let her body give in. For reasons that made no sense, Eliza wanted to take care of her. And damn, she was good at it. "Mmm-hmm," she murmured. She heated under Eliza's touch. Eliza was warm and gentle. Mia melted into her strong arms and soft breaths and gentle tugs in her hair.

Mia fidgeted a bit more, finding her comfortable spot.

"All settled?" Eliza asked.

"Think so."

"Good night, Mia," Eliza said.

Mia placed one arm across Eliza's stomach and closed her eyes. "Good night, Eliza." And then she fell asleep.

Eliza

Sunlight filtered through the gauzy curtains leading to the balcony at the far wall of Eliza's suite. Eliza was struck with a sense of panic that this was the first time she's woken up all week when it wasn't dark outside.

It took her a few moments to realize that last night wasn't a dream. That Mia really did show up at her door and then curl up against her like a sleepy cat. She was still there now, her auburn curls splayed out against the pillow and Eliza's arm.

God, had Eliza really suggested they sleep together? This was getting messy. Too messy. Mia needed her to keep this ruse going and here she was asking her to sleep in her bed. And worse, she hadn't even gotten work done last night.

Mia rolled over in her sleep state and nuzzled into Eliza's neck. Eliza froze. It tickled and it made Eliza feel all kinds of desire. Heat and want pooled inside her. But most of all, Eliza felt an overwhelming urge to roll over, pull Mia in close and never let go. She had been able to provide comfort for Mia. And she wondered, just for a moment, what it might be like to do this every morning.

Mia snuggled in even closer, and Eliza had to fight every instinct in her body to not pepper Mia's jawline with kisses and pull her close. That would be a terrible idea. It would make things even messier than they already were.

Instead, she gently stroked her arm and whispered, "Mia?"

No response. Mia let out a little snore and rolled the other way. So she'd been asleep. That was probably for the best. Eliza untangled her arm from below Mia and sneaked out from her bed. She spent a few minutes freshening up in the bathroom before sitting down at the outdoor table with her coffee and her laptop.

She had no idea if Mia was the kind of person who would be mad that Eliza didn't wake her up to run, but she wasn't about to bother her. Eliza made quick work of her emails. Eliza was damn good at her job. Within an hour she had put out three fires, responded to an ungodly number of emails, set up a meeting with the editor who had listened to her father and mapped out their third-quarter plans.

And she hadn't needed her father to do it. For good measure, she drafted three memos to her teams, copying her father on all of them, directing all questions to come to her specifically and noting that under no circumstances should any photographs of Mia Knowles appear in any publication until further notice.

There. She couldn't undo the past, but she could at least guarantee that little bit of privacy for Mia moving forward. If she didn't want to be in the public eye, then she wouldn't be.

"Morning."

Mia's voice came from somewhere behind her, and Eliza froze before realizing she'd been in some kind of work trance. Mia set a huge mug of coffee next to the cold, half-empty one next to Eliza's laptop.

Eliza smiled at the cup. "Did I wake you with my typing? Sometimes I get carried away."

Mia giggled. "No, but I'm no longer curious what hyperfocused Eliza looks like." She pointed at the chair opposite Eliza and waited for Eliza to nod before she sat. "I've been up for a bit. I asked you if you wanted coffee twice, but you were like—" she mimed typing "—really into it."

"Sorry, it happens. Thanks for this." Eliza took a sip of the coffee. It was hot and just a bit sweet. "How did you know how I take my coffee?"

Mia sipped at her own. "Well, if the eighty-seven sugar packets on the counter didn't give it away, it might have been watching you at brunch yesterday. You're not so hard to figure out, Eliza Brewer."

Eliza's chest tightened. There was something about hearing her name on Mia's lips that made her want to see what else her mouth could do. "So," she began and cleared her throat, "do you have plans before the bachelorette party tonight?"

Mia huffed. "Unfortunately. My parents want to…" Mia made air quotes and sighed.

"Have a meeting with you?"

Eliza felt a fierce protectiveness come over her. She closed her laptop and stared at Mia across the table. Beyond her, the sea stretched out before them. Eliza could still see the path Mia ran early the first morning. She could still remember watching her as her feet dug into the sand. She was so strong, so confident. Eliza wanted to remind her of who she could be.

"What if you already had plans?" she asked.

Mia blinked. "What did you have in mind?"

"Well, I'm just saying, I'm caught up on work stuff for the moment. Maybe your girlfriend swept you away somewhere without warning. And we lost track of time. Somewhere we can't be found."

"I can't just ignore them." Mia bit the edge

of her lip and frowned. "I need them to listen to me. Maybe it's going to be a good meeting?"

Eliza raised a brow in question and Mia huffed. "Fine. I know it's not a good meeting."

"I'm not saying ignore them. Just…delay the meeting. Give yourself some time to calm down. Give yourself some space to figure out what you want to say. Come spend the day with me instead. Let's give you some time to get ready for your big pitch."

A smile spread slowly across Mia's face. "Not ignoring them. Mentally preparing. That makes sense, actually."

"And by the time we got back, it would be too late. Put it off until tomorrow. We have plans tonight anyway. You can't fall down on your maid-of-honor duties. And I'm the best woman and all. We'll be much too busy."

"Very busy."

"So, what do you say, Knowles? Want to go off grid with me?"

By the time they'd made it down to the beach all of the kayaks and paddleboards had been laid out for use. Mia fidgeted nervously beside her. Maybe Eliza had read the situation wrong. What if Mia would have preferred her to charter a small boat? Or maybe just hide in a grotto somewhere?

"I've never paddleboarded before," Mia admitted. "Do you have any other options?"

"Of course," the man said jovially. He motioned to a group of boards in varying length. "If you're nervous about paddleboarding, let your girlfriend help. Take this board for two."

Mia's skin went adorably pink along her cheekbones and between her breasts. And now *Eliza* was staring at *her* breasts. Eliza swallowed thickly, then entwined their fingers and tugged.

"Come on, Mia. It will be fine. I've got you."

And it was as if those three words held some kind of magic between them.

Eliza didn't have time to overthink it or worry or analyze the potential outcomes. She just locked their personal belongings into a locker and waded into the water after Mia. It wasn't until they were both seated, legs dangling in the ocean, facing each other straddled on the paddle board that Mia asked, "Now what?"

Eliza smirked. "Well, now we stand up and try to see how far we can go before our legs get tired or our arms get tired—or both."

"That all sounds really great, except for the standing-up part." Mia wiggled her hips and the board teetered from side to side.

"It's going to be fine. Watch." Eliza pulled her legs up onto the board and handed her paddle to Mia before standing up. Mia gazed up at her, the sun a halo behind her head. "See? Now you do it."

Mia grimaced. "I'm not so sure you want that. I'm less of a liability when I'm seated. Right here." She patted the board on either side.

"We have to paddle," Eliza said, a small hint of exasperation in her voice. But Mia wouldn't budge. She crossed her arms and raised a brow and pouted at the front half of the paddleboard.

"Fine," Eliza laughed. "You win. For now. At least turn around and enjoy the view."

Eliza didn't get out in nature much, but when she did, she spent time paddleboarding with friends on the Hudson River. Years of summers on the river gave her the core and arm strength to get both of them to the grotto beyond the open waters of the beach.

Mia was adorable sitting cross-legged on the board. She dipped her fingers into the water, letting it flow around her, and often tipped her closed eyes to the golden sun. This was how Eliza was going to remember Mia in the coming months. Smiling and full of wonder, the sun pulling out the smattering of freckles on her shoulders even more.

"Okay, we're here."

Mia opened her eyes. The alcove gave them the privacy Eliza so desperately craved.

Mia looked around the high walls of the craggy rock and the still waters. "Where are we?" she asked softly. She dipped her fingers into the sea, which was now a navy blue.

"Somewhere no one can find us," Eliza said. Her smile spread out across her face. "And now you're going to try this for real."

She leaned down and reached out a hand. Mia grumbled, but she still let Eliza take her hand.

"Don't let go, okay?" Mia asked.

"I promise." Eliza squeezed her hands and centered her weight, ready to be there for Mia if she needed her.

The board wobbled, and they almost fell twice, but suddenly, miraculously, Mia found herself standing on the board. She let out a laugh, disbelief clear in her eyes.

"See, I knew you could do it."

Their bodies were flush against each other. Mia's mouth was centimeters from hers. Her hair was frizzy from the salt in the air. Between the sun and the curls, Mia looked like fire itself. Like life itself dancing in front of her.

Eliza leaned in and closed her eyes.

"Maybe we..." Mia trailed off and Eliza froze. Both of their breaths were heaving. "I just. Maybe we shouldn't?"

Eliza blew out a breath and pressed her forehead into Mia's. She nodded. "You're right.

Of course you're right. I'm sorry. I got carried away. It won't happen again."

"It's not that I don't—"

"Mia, it's fine. I promise. Let's get back to the shore. I think we only have seven hours before the bachelorette party tonight and you have to help paddle. We might need all the time we can get."

Mia fixed her with a look. "Very funny, Brewer."

Eliza groaned internally. When Mia used her last name it made her want to take back every promise she'd made herself about this week.

"Come on, let's start planning." Eliza knew they were pushing their luck staying out here so long. She wanted to distract Mia, not make things worse for her with her parents. So they needed to get down to business. "We're going to brainstorm a thousand ways to make sure your conversation with your parents goes the way *you* want it to."

"You'd do that for me?" Mia looked up at her with wide eyes, her lashes a million miles long and something like hope sparking to life beneath the surface.

Eliza's heart clenched. "I'll do that *with* you," she replied. "You've got this."

"Yeah?"

"Yeah."

"Thank you for this. For last night. For today. For helping me get out of my own head. I had a lot of fun. And I didn't even fall in."

Mia turned to face the right direction and looked back; arm outstretched for a paddle. She clutched it in her hands and smirked at Eliza, full of confidence.

And then Mia Knowles fell into the water. And Eliza had no choice but to jump in, too.

CHAPTER TEN

Mia

THE NIGHT WAS a glimmering haze of lights and laughter, spilling from the crowded streets of Taormina. It was as if the whole city had come alive to celebrate with them, a pulse of energy thrumming through the air as the wedding party stepped into the restaurant—a hidden gem on the edge of the nightlife district. Mia felt a thrill of satisfaction with how things had turned out. This was the one thing she'd planned on her own for her friend's wedding, a special gift for Cate and Noah with all their favorite things: delicious food, their closest friends and plans for dancing.

Lots of dancing.

A string of tiny lights twinkled overhead on the terrace, competing with the stars, casting a warm, honeyed glow over tables draped in crisp linens and rich velvet chairs. It felt like the type of place she'd bring a date on her own, secluded and romantic and tucked away.

Eliza seemed to like the place as well. She raised one brow at Mia and gave a nod of approval.

"Well done," Eliza mouthed as she followed the hostess.

A thrill ran down Mia's spine at the compliment. The place felt like a secret kept just for them, a glamorous oasis surrounded by the lively hum of the city.

As they were led to their table on the edge of the terrace, Mia felt the cool evening breeze sweep in from the sea, carrying with it a hint of salt and jasmine. Around her, her friends' voices rose in excitement, bubbling over with anticipation for the night ahead. This was Cate's last night of freedom—*her* bachelorette party—and Mia had worked tirelessly to make sure it was perfect, booking them the best view in Sicily, where they could feel the city's heartbeat mingling with the rush of the waves below.

But it felt a bit like Mia's night, too. Eliza stuck close to her side, a reminder of their day together, hiding away from the world. Eliza had been there for her, protected her the best she could. Mia's shoulders still felt warm from the afternoon sun heating their skin as they floated knee to knee on the paddleboard.

Mia pushed the memory from her mind. She needed to focus on Cate tonight, but she couldn't stop staring at Eliza's toned shoulders beneath her jacket. Now she knew what those shoulders looked like when they were being worked. She only peeked when Eliza wasn't looking back at her and *only* for a few seconds. Ever since Eliza pulled Mia from the water this afternoon, her muscled arms straining to right her on the board, Mia couldn't seem to focus on anything else.

"Mia. I said, did your parents find you?" Beth quirked a brow at Mia and waited. How many times had she asked that question? Was Mia really that distracted? "They were looking for you this morning down by the pool."

Beth's subtle frown and perfect posture gave an air of indifference. But it no doubt brought her joy to remind Mia of how she was constantly under her parents' thumb.

"Oh, really?" Mia responded, nonplussed. "I saw them for a moment before heading out tonight. I'm sure it wasn't anything important."

It had, in fact, been important. At least to her parents. She'd been trying to shake off the conversation for the last hour. They'd cornered her the moment she returned from her ocean escape and told her she needed to stop seeing Eliza Brewer. Immediately.

"I thought this is what you wanted?" She'd thrown the words back in their faces. "Don't you want me splashing my life all over the gossip columns?"

"Not. Like. *This*. I'm sure Eliza is lovely," her father said. "But she isn't your match. Why don't you date Beth again? Or maybe someone from my board? Brewer Enterprises is not going to expand our family name. She isn't even in our same circles. We don't ask much from you, Mia. And surely you can understand that Eliza is going to bring you down."

How could they say these things about Eliza? They didn't even know her! Anger burned behind her eyes and she tried to keep her voice from shaking. "She was at the Fieldings' fundraiser," Mia interrupted without thinking.

"Yes," her mother finally spoke. But it wasn't to defend her daughter. "I remember quite clearly." Mia blushed at the memory of how their first encounter was interrupted by her mother. Mia wished she could go back in time and restart things with Eliza.

Wait. No, she didn't. There wasn't anything to *start* with Eliza. Was there? She pushed away the thought and tried to process the words of her father swirling around her like likes and comments and shares on her social media.

"This ends now, Mia," her father rasped. "We

can talk in the morning. I know you need to get to the party. But please, be reasonable. We need you to be seen with someone who can improve our brand, build on it. She's older than you, Mia. And she seems boring."

"Don't talk about my girlfriend that way," Mia had practically shouted. "I'm leaving."

And then she was out the door. She'd never, never spoken to her parents that way. But the more they talked about Eliza, the more she wanted to burn it all down. Eliza was brilliant. And gorgeous. And generous. She was so many things. Anyone would be lucky to date her.

I'd *be lucky to date her*.

The thought hit her so quickly she wasn't sure what to do. Because technically, yes, everyone thought she was dating Eliza Brewer. But now Mia couldn't stop thinking about what this would all be like if it was real. If Eliza truly did like her in the way they were pretending.

The memory of Eliza leaning toward her on the paddleboard, water droplets glistening on her warm brown skin, came rushing back, sending goose bumps down Mia's arms. Eliza would have kissed her. She'd known it. And there'd been no one there to see them.

A kiss like that? A kiss just between the two of them when it might mean something. Mia couldn't handle that. She couldn't let herself give in to the fantasy that she could actually date someone as accomplished and confident and gorgeous as Eliza Brewer. And God, she *was* gorgeous. So Mia had pulled away.

Even if she really, really wanted Eliza to try again.

And now she had Eliza just inches away from her on the terrace of a romantic restaurant while Beth stared at her from across the table. A reminder of what she once had and no longer wanted.

Mia felt nothing for Beth at all. Not even annoyance, just complete indifference. She didn't want to make her jealous; she didn't want to make her regret dumping Mia. Mia wanted absolutely nothing from her at all.

"Thanks for letting me know, Beth. I appreciate it." Mia gave her a genuine smile and Beth returned it. Even if she looked somewhat confused. "I'll catch up with you tomorrow, at the rehearsal dinner, okay?"

She leaned over and squeezed Eliza's thigh. A silent thank-you for being here that she wasn't sure she conveyed correctly. Eliza looked down at Mia's hand in confusion. And fair. Mia wished she hadn't backed away from that almost kiss on the paddleboard.

Mia wasn't interested in fake kisses anymore. She was only interested in seeing if this thing with Eliza could be real. God, she should have just kissed her. Given in to this desire building in her, even if it could only last a few more days. She was done trying to position herself as the perfect, responsible daughter. Nothing she did was good enough. She might as well do whatever she wanted instead.

A slow, sad song began playing from the other side of the restaurant. A guitar softly strummed while a woman's voice rang out in mournful Italian. The emotion of it hit Mia in her heart. She didn't know anything past conversational Italian, but whatever this woman was singing about, Mia felt it. It was full of want and need and loss.

Mia turned into Eliza and whispered near the shell of her ear, "Dance with me?"

She needed to get her hands on Eliza. Or rather, she needed Eliza's hands on her. On the safety of the dance floor, Mia could show Eliza how she felt even if she couldn't say it out loud. She could give in, just a little, just for the moment. She wanted to bury her face in the crook of Eliza's neck and breathe in her musky scent. She needed to memorize it for later when it wouldn't be so readily available.

Eliza's eyes narrowed as she considered Mia's question. "Later at the club? Sure."

"No. Now." Mia gestured to the makeshift

dance floor just inside the restaurant. A scattering of couples swayed to the music, arms draped over each other moving gracefully and slowly.

"No," Eliza said in a hushed voice. "We can't do that. We're finishing dinner and then we have another stop."

"I'm not really interested in what we should or should not be doing." Mia's thumb began a long, slow path up Eliza's thigh. Eliza's breath hitched as she stared at Mia's hand. She sucked her bottom lip into her mouth.

"You're not?" she asked, never taking her eyes away from Mia's hand.

"Dance with me. Please."

Eliza nodded and Mia stood, holding out her hand. Mia's heart thundered in her chest as their friends cat-called and whistled as they walked to the dance floor. Cate was incorrigible, all decked out in her white minidress and vintage veil. Mia gripped Eliza's hand tighter and led her to the center of the room.

Eliza wrapped her arms around Mia and she melted into them. There was just something about being in Eliza's arms. So strong and safe and Mia knew nothing bad could happen if she was in them. She was stronger for it.

They began to sway slowly to the strum of the guitar. After a moment, Eliza's soft whisper broke through. "Why did you ask me to dance?"

Mia rested her head on Eliza's shoulder, breathing in her perfume and the linen of her jacket. "Because I like you like this."

"Like this?"

"Yeah, focused. Concentrating. Like you can't think about anything else because this is taking up too much space."

Eliza huffed. "You're already taking up all the space lately." Mia let the words sink in.

She rested her head on Eliza's shoulder and nuzzled into her neck. She vaguely registered that Cate and Noah were on the dance floor now. And a few other friends, too. She closed her eyes and pressed her hips against Eliza's and pretended for a moment they were together. Eliza's body was rounded and soft and pressed back into Mia, meeting her at every point. The feeling was so warm and delicious and felt so right.

And then it was gone.

"I'm sorry, I can't…" Eliza loosened her grip and stared down at Mia. Her eyes were wide and full of confusion. "I can't do this. I'm sorry."

And then she was gone, retreating out the back door of the restaurant. Panic climbed up the back of Mia's neck. Maybe she'd gone too far. Maybe Eliza was still upset from earlier. *This is what happens when Mia tries. She gets rejected.*

Mia scrunched her nose at Cate in an *I'm not sure* look and pointed toward the back of the building. She mouthed, "I'll check on her."

It didn't take long to find Eliza. She was leaning against the wall in an otherwise empty alley. Her eyes were closed and her hands were fisted at her sides.

"Eliza, what's wrong?"

"Please, Mia. Just leave me alone." The words were quiet and hollow in the small space. Mia fought against her urge to listen, her urge to back off and comply.

"Absolutely not. Tell me what's wrong. We were just in there dancing and then you…you run out?"

"What else was I supposed to do?" Anger flashed hot in her eyes. Eliza's eyes were wide, pupils blown black, and her breath was ragged. "I can't dance with you, Mia. I can't hold you and feel your breath on my neck and your hair in my fingers. I can't do all that and not imagine what it might be like to touch you. To kiss you. To wreck you. I know I said I could do this, but I can't. Not like that."

Eliza took a step forward and placed one hand under Mia's jaw. She threaded the fingers of her other hand through her curls. Mia couldn't move. Couldn't breathe. She was caught in the trance of Eliza's words, her hungry stare, and the way her full lips could barely get the words out. "I can't keep looking at you and pretend I don't feel anything. It's too hard to kiss you, or touch you, and know I can't have you the way I want."

Mia sucked in a breath. Eliza *wanted* her. She could see it in the way her jaw clenched. In the way her eyes were full of heat. The way her fingers were now cradling Mia's face, so gentle and yet so determined. Mia felt drunk with this new information. She hadn't expected this at all. Her own desires mirrored so clearly in the way Eliza was staring at her.

"And what way is that?" Mia whispered. She stared back at Eliza, matching her furious glare, matching her anger and frustration and desire. "Show me, Brewer. How do you want me?"

Eliza surged forward and pressed her mouth to Mia's. It was an angry kiss. Nothing hesitant or tentative. Just pure need as she tugged on Mia's lower lip and pressed their bodies as close as they could be. It was pleasure and pain and Mia felt the drop in her stomach as the inevitable finally caught up with them.

Eliza turned them and pushed Mia against the wall. She liked the sting of the stucco and the way Eliza's arms caged her in. Mia broke the kiss and panted into Eliza's mouth. She needed to be sure. She needed to see Eliza's eyes.

But then Eliza slid one leg between Mia's thighs and groaned before kissing her again.

This time the kiss was slower, but just as needy. And when Mia opened her mouth slightly, Eliza's tongue found hers, sliding along the edge and igniting a storm of desire inside Mia's chest. Mia felt the kiss everywhere, arousal pooling low in her belly, a shiver of pleasure running up her legs to the point where Eliza pressed against her.

There was no one to see this. No one to convince this was real. Just the two of them, in a dark alley, with nothing but the moon, the distant sounds of the musicians and Eliza's mouth asking her for more.

Eliza

Eliza was usually in control. She was good at being in control. She didn't let her emotions get the best of her and she certainly didn't go around kissing beautiful women in alleys. It seemed as if everything Eliza held true to in life was upending itself this week. Her father undermining her work, her employees listening to him even though she was supposed to be the one in charge. Eliza was losing control.

And if everything had already spiraled this far, she might as well enjoy the chaos before she had to right it all. She could spend the next few minutes, the next few hours, the next few days, giving in to all her desires. She could have Mia, in whatever messy way Mia would have her. She was done trying to keep herself stable this week.

"I need to get you out of here," Eliza hummed into Mia's neck. She ran her nose down the edge of her jaw and kissed her under her chin. "I need to get you back to my room. *Now*."

Mia froze, her eyes wide and wild. Eliza had gone too far. Pushed too much. Perhaps Mia didn't want *that*. That *much*. Eliza shook her head, ready to walk back the offer. She opened her mouth to take it back when Mia's fingers dug hard into Eliza's hips and Mia pulled her closer.

Mia let out a low moan, a plea. "Yes. Please." It may as well have been a growl. "Last night was torture. Lying right next to you and not being able to touch you."

God, Mia had a way with words. She was so quiet, except when she wasn't. Eliza wondered if having sex with Mia would be like this, too. Would she ask for what she wanted? Would she tell Eliza exactly what to do? A thrill went down Eliza's spine. And that excitement must have been why her hand trailed up Mia's inner thigh. Mia's words caught in her throat. She swallowed thickly and nodded once, her eyes hooded and dark.

It felt so good to leave Mia at a loss for words.

Eliza's hand trailed higher, under Mia's skirt, and was rewarded with a hitch in Mia's breath when she found the silky softness of her underwear, already damp. Eliza took her time, slowly moving her hand, cupping Mia's sex where she wanted her most.

Eliza pressed her lips to Mia's again, drowning out a moan. Mia opened for her, allowing Eliza to slip her tongue inside and kiss into Mia's mouth. Their kiss on the dance floor two nights ago had been for show. It was hot and rushed and full of fire. Their small touches and brief kisses since then had been a whisper of what was possible.

But this kiss was just for them. It wasn't about convincing their families, or mutually beneficial career moves. This was Mia opening herself up to Eliza, exposing herself in a way Eliza wasn't sure she deserved. But she wanted it—whatever Mia would give her—for the next few days.

Eliza wanted her naked; she wanted to watch her unravel, but first she wanted to see what other moans she could coax out of Mia in this alley.

Mia dropped her thigh to one side, shifting the fabric just enough to give Eliza the access she was so desperately seeking.

"Please," Mia sighed.

Eliza slid her hand higher and was rewarded with Mia's low breaths coming faster and faster. Eliza wanted to take her time. Mia deserved attention and care. But when she began moving against Eliza's fingers, meeting her with each pass, Eliza gave Mia exactly what she was seeking.

A loud smack rang out in the alley, soon followed by the low chuckle that could only belong to Noah Brewer.

"Dammit," Eliza muttered, pulling her hand down and away just in time before she caught her brother's shocked face in her periphery. He likely hadn't seen anything specific, but Eliza definitely had a flushed Mia pressed against a wall. She held her hand behind her back.

"So, we're heading over to the club now." He put one hand on the back of his neck and didn't look Eliza in the eyes. The last time Eliza had a girlfriend, Noah had been a kid. He'd never seen her like this and clearly, he was just as embarrassed as she was.

"We'll be right there." Mia's voice was a squeak.

Eliza flattened out her shirt, which had somehow come untucked from her pants, and then decided messing with it would only be more incriminating. She dropped the hem and nodded at her brother.

"Yup, we'll be right behind you."

"Sounds good," he said, already turning and walking back toward the restaurant. Just before the door closed, she could hear him mutter, "This is the last time Cate sends me to check on my sister."

The door clicked shut and Eliza closed her eyes. There was a part of her that wanted to go after her brother. She wanted to make sure he would not tell their father and that he wouldn't say anything to Cate. There was a part of her that—

The sound of stifled giggles interrupted her thoughts. She turned to find Mia with her lips pressed together, trying to hold in a laugh.

"You look like you're sixteen and just got caught with a girl in your room."

"Well, good." Eliza blew out a breath. "I *feel* like I'm sixteen and just got caught with a girl in my room."

Mia pushed off from the wall and sighed.

"We can't just go, can we? Skip the rest of the night?" Eliza tried to make her voice calm. But she'd just had her hand up Mia's skirt and she was still breathless.

"Damn, I wish we could." Mia's heated gaze roamed over Eliza. She felt herself go warm everywhere all at once. "We have to go with them, though. I planned tonight." She felt like the entire world had tipped on its axis, and here Mia was promising they'd go back to the party.

"Fine," Eliza huffed.

"It's going to be okay," Mia said. She leaned close and whispered in Eliza's ear. Her warm breath tickled. "But you're going to have to spend the rest of the night knowing how much I want you. And knowing that tonight, when we go back to the hotel, I'll be going to your room."

She walked past Eliza, her skirt perfectly hugging her hips as she pulled the door halfway open.

"Eliza? Are you coming?" Mia asked, her voice completely innocent.

"This night is going to be torture." Eliza rolled her eyes, but followed behind.

"I'm counting on it," Mia said, smirking and lacing her fingers through Eliza's before pulling her back into the party.

CHAPTER ELEVEN

Mia

THE NIGHT HAD in fact been torture. Kissing Eliza in the alley, when no one was there to watch, made something snap inside Mia. Now that she knew, she *knew*, how much Eliza wanted her, it was as if she'd jumped out of an airplane and had to spend the rest of the night in a free fall. The only thing keeping her focused was the knowledge that Eliza had promised, at some point later that evening, to pull the rip cord and open the parachute that would bring them both down together. And she had every intention of holding her to it.

Mia endured knowing looks from Beth, a wink from Cate and Noah's stammering and refusal to look her in the eye. But it had all been worth it, because at precisely 11:02 p.m., Eliza stifled a yawn and claimed, "I can't keep up with you young people. I'm turning in for the night." Then she'd stood, smoothed out her wide leg pants that clung to her generous hips and turned to Mia. "Are you coming? Or should I catch up with you later?"

Mia stood fast, and the edge of her knee hit the table and knocked over an empty glass. "I can come with you." And then she'd had to listen to giggles as they'd made their escape into the night.

It had been so easy, in the dark alley, with Eliza's hand up her skirt making her a useless puddle of want and desire to give in to whatever this was. Eliza told her she wanted her. Not that she had feelings for her. Not that she *liked* Mia. But that she felt the same burning attraction.

She'd told Mia she couldn't be near her and not want this. But it was different now, three hours later, when they'd had a chance to think it all through. Perhaps Eliza had changed her mind? Maybe she really was tired. The ride in the town car was excruciating. A thousand little looks and small touches, but not words. Not anything of consequence. Which was fine. Mia was done talking.

But Eliza's hand never left Mia's as they made their way to Eliza's suite. The small of Mia's back, the edge of her hip, playing with the hairs that had come loose on the back of her neck in the cab. Eliza held onto Mia like she might disappear if she didn't. She held onto Mia like it meant something.

For maybe the second time in her life, Mia was doing something because she wanted to, not because she was supposed to. Kissing Eliza, being with Eliza, was a choice all her own. And it was a good one. It was this realization, even more than the lust stirring in her body anytime Eliza's fingers brushed against her, that made her realize this was the right choice. She felt it deep in her bones. The same feeling she'd had when she'd insisted on going to grad school. An inexplicable knowledge that this was going to change her life for the better.

She wanted Eliza. And she was going to give Eliza anything she wanted.

But Eliza didn't hurry. Nothing about Eliza was ever fevered or rushed. Mia found it both annoying and thrilling that Eliza had so much patience. Eliza set down her bag and took Mia's from her shoulder, gently placing it on the entry table. Mia shivered at the feeling of Eliza's fingers against her shoulder.

Eliza walked toward the expansive wall of windows looking out over the ocean. She pulled open the French doors, letting the late-night breeze fill the room. Mia, feeling emboldened by the kiss in the alley and the tension of the car, approached Eliza from behind and wrapped her arms around Eliza's waist. Mia bit down gently on the edge of Eliza's shoulder and smoothed it over with a soft kiss. A test. A kiss in the privacy of the room. The slight graze of her teeth silently asking Eliza just how far she wanted to take this tonight.

Eliza tipped her head back onto Mia's shoulder, exposing her neck and inviting Mia's mouth to explore. Mia took her time exploring this small opening from Eliza. Eliza who was always so buttoned up, so closed off, was pliant and soft in her arms now. Mia murmured into her neck as she kissed along her jawline.

"You are absolutely beautiful, Eliza. The way you move against me. You've been driving me wild all night."

Mia didn't usually talk like this. So openly about what she wanted. But there was no denying this any longer. She wanted Eliza. And if Eliza wanted this, too, she didn't want to waste another minute.

As if Eliza could read her thoughts, she spun and sealed her mouth over Mia's completely. Eliza pushed Mia against the wall, and nuzzled into her neck, humming. "That." She ran her nose along Mia's jawline. "Was." A kiss behind her ear. "Torture."

Eliza's breath tickled Mia's neck and she giggled. Eliza caught the laughter in her mouth, capturing Mia's lips with her own. All thoughts of confessing her feelings to Eliza flew out of her brain. There would be time for that later. Eliza's eyes were hooded and hungry and Mia was intent on giving her whatever she needed.

"What do you want?" Mia asked, a gasp escaping her mouth as Eliza continued to explore Mia's body. Her mouth ran along Mia's shoulder and she bit down at the edge, a sharp pain that made the soft brush of her tongue that much sweeter. Apparently, Eliza was great at payback.

"Anything," Eliza whispered against her neck.

That one word sent a thrill down Mia's spine. Eliza had been reduced to single words, incoherent ones at that. Eliza could command boardrooms and run entire companies, but now she was a mess. Her eyes were hooded and desperate. "Please. Anything." She closed her eyes and seemed to give something up. Hand something over to Mia.

Mia grabbed at one of Eliza's exploring hands and brought it to her mouth. She kissed her fingertips before pulling two of them into her mouth.

"I trust you," Eliza said with a hiss when Mia scraped her teeth along Eliza's fingers.

It was everything Mia didn't realize she needed to hear. Eliza Brewer trusted her. Wanted her. Mia wasn't going to waste a second.

"Follow me," Mia whispered. She pulled Eliza into the bedroom and sat her down on the edge of the bed. She undid the clasp on Eliza's shoes, sliding first one then the other from her feet.

She ran her hands up Eliza's legs. And Eliza let her. She watched her, kiss drunk and desperate to be touched.

Mia took her time. She removed Eliza's watch. Her earrings were next as Mia placed a kiss behind each earlobe. She took Eliza Brewer apart, piece by piece. Her tank top was next and the thin black lace of her bra made Mia stumble. God, she was gorgeous, her nipples already straining against the fabric. Mia wanted to capture each one in her mouth, so she did. She laid Eliza back on the bed and teased each one through the lace. Eliza squirmed and sighed and breathed out a "yes" and "more" and "please."

Had Eliza ever once in her life begged for something? Mia wanted to see what else she could get that mouth to do.

"You're doing so well," Mia said. She positioned herself over Eliza's gorgeous body, a perfect blend of softness and strength. She continued kissing her way up from her neck and into her mouth. "I've got you."

And then Mia stripped off her own shirt.

Eliza

Eliza couldn't remember another moment when she'd felt this vulnerable and this safe all at once. Mia looked down at her with adoring eyes as if Eliza was something to be treasured, someone to be treasured. Mia looked at her like Eliza was worthy just by existing. She didn't want anything more from her than that.

Eliza swallowed thickly and pushed back the emotions building inside her. This was just sex. This was Mia blowing off some steam. The sexual tension between them was palpable. It had been for days. It had been since the moment they first spoke back at the Fieldings' fundraiser. Eliza was going to let Mia take her fill. She'd give her whatever she wanted in this bed and ignore everything else.

"What do you need?" Mia trailed her fingers down Eliza's ribs and then leaned down, hovering over her. Her auburn curls blanketed either side of Eliza's face. "I want to make you feel good."

"This—" Eliza's voice broke off, shaking. She closed her eyes and tried again. "This. You. All of this. Just keep touching me."

Mia quirked a soft smile down at Eliza. She must have seen something there because she didn't push anymore. She took her time exploring every inch of Eliza. It felt like seconds or maybe hours before she had Eliza wrung out and begging.

Eliza had slept with other women before. Granted, it had been a while. A long while. But she knew the mechanics. She knew what to do. But Mia made every touch, every caress, feel like something breakable and brand-new. She'd never been with another person *like this*. She'd never felt so all consumed before.

Whatever Eliza had been holding onto, whatever restraint she had left inside her, she let it go. With each touch from Mia, with each murmured word of encouragement, she let her walls fall away. Soon she was trembling and grasping for her and the hot prick of tears took over her eyes.

"Baby, are you okay?" Mia was there in an instant, brushing away one traitorous tear. Her lips were swollen and her eyes were wild with concern. Eliza couldn't speak. She took Mia's face in her hands and kissed her. She could taste herself and the mess Mia had made of her. She nodded into the kiss, deepening it. Mia let her take control. She gave it all back to her.

Eliza knew what to do with this. "Lay back," she demanded. "Please. I want to see all of you. I want to take care of you now."

Eliza practically growled when Mia's mouth dropped open in shock and then snapped closed. Her eyes darkened to a rich umber and she nodded before falling back onto the pillow.

Later, when the light had shifted in the room from darkness to some kind of early-morning gray, Mia draped an arm across Eliza's stomach and nuzzled into her neck. Eliza gripped Mia's hip and ran her thumb over a small mark on her skin.

"What's this?" she whispered into Mia's hair.

"Birthmark," Mia murmured. "I kind of think it looks like an island."

Eliza palmed that patch of skin and considered. "I can see it," she agreed. "Like a tiny Sicily, right there on your hip."

Eliza pulled Mia's leg up so it crossed over hers. "And this?" She brushed her fingers along the edge of Mia's knee. There was a scar there, though she couldn't see it now. She'd noticed it the first night out on the terrace. A small patch of skin that looked healed over ten times.

"Hazard of running." Mia nuzzled in closer and closed her eyes. "I tripped on a rock on a trail near my house. It wasn't pretty. I had to limp back and I was already a few miles down the trail."

Worry flooded Eliza. She didn't like the idea of Mia having to rescue herself. But somehow the image didn't surprise her. Mia wasn't one to shy away from a challenge.

"But you kept running?" Eliza asked. "Even after that."

Mia smiled into Eliza's neck. "You say it like I was hospitalized. Runners get hurt all the time. You should see me after a race. I'm a mess."

"I'd like that."

There was a beat of silence. And Eliza realized she'd said that part out loud. She bit the edge of her mouth. Those words implied a future. A moment after this week when maybe they'd still see each other. She considered taking the words back. Making a joke.

But Mia sat up on one elbow and kissed Eliza. "Only if you run with me." She kissed her again.

Eliza knew Mia was joking, but her heart clenched a little at the idea of waiting for Mia at the end of a finish line with a towel or a water.

"Not a chance in hell," Eliza said against Mia's mouth. "I'll stick to paddleboards, thank you very much."

Mia dug her fingers into Eliza's hip and tickled, distracting Eliza and causing her to yelp. Mia took the opportunity to cover Eliza in kisses from her mouth to her collarbone to the spot between her breasts. It was heaven, watching Mia enjoy her.

God, this woman was everything. Silly and romantic and raw and honest and brave. Mia had crescent-moon indents from Eliza's fingernails just above her hips, a birthmark above her right hip bone and a tiny scar on her left knee. Eliza cataloged each mark of her skin and committed it to memory.

"You're ridiculous," she said when Mia was

satisfied with her teasing and collapsed back into Eliza's arms.

"I know," Mia said. And Eliza couldn't be sure if Mia meant it as a joke or not. She pulled her close and tugged the blanket up around them. "But you like it."

I really do.

Eliza trailed her fingers up and down Mia's back in a slow rhythm. Eventually, Mia's breath shifted and Eliza knew she was asleep. She knew next week this would be a memory, something she could look back on when she was still in her office late at night, or hopefully something she could fill her dreams with. So she committed it all to memory.

Because that's what Mia Knowles was. A dream. Someone who deserved the whole entire world. Someone who deserved a partner and a cheerleader and someone who could be with her and be present.

She deserved better than a woman six years older than her who was always at her work's—and her father's—beck and call. Someone who couldn't even admit that she wanted a relationship. What kind of life could she really give Mia? Her fingers stopped mid-motion as her own thoughts echoed back at her. It was the first time she'd admitted, even if it was only to herself, that she wanted *more* than what she'd had the last few years.

Her mother's words echoed in her brain. *His dreams don't have to be yours. And his pressure has no place on your back.* Eliza was used to the pressure at work. She was good at holding that burden. Especially knowing it was not something Noah could handle. Definitely something their mother hadn't been able to handle.

Even if there was a world where Mia Knowles wanted Eliza, wanted all of her, including the messy parts she didn't show to others, there was no one else to take on the responsibilities she had to her family. To her career. This was to protect her brother. Support her mother. Give them stability and draw the attention away from them. She needed to keep her father focused on her and the company.

Eliza blew out a breath as tears pricked at the edge of her eyes. This was for the best. She'd take this week with Mia. This dream week, full of secret kisses, and laughter in the sunshine, and even the godforsaken gondola ride, and tuck them safely away. As far as Mia knew, this was a purely physical attraction. And it had to stay this way.

This ended here. It ended in Sicily.

Eliza pressed her eyes shut tight and let her breaths mimic Mia's. If she only had this one night, she wasn't going to dwell on what she was losing. She pulled Mia close, pressed a kiss into her hair and fell asleep easily and peacefully, perhaps for the first time, as Mia held her close.

CHAPTER TWELVE

Mia

MIA WOKE SOMETIME before dawn, her mind racing and her body aching for a run. Her shoulders were cold, and the blanket had fallen away as it usually did. She reached, half-asleep, for the covers and instead found Eliza's soft stomach, warm and inviting.

A lump formed in Mia's throat as she pushed herself closer to Eliza. Mia loved watching her exhale soft puffs of breath into the quiet room. She looked so at peace. Mia didn't want to disturb her, but she couldn't help creeping closer and burrowing her face into the crook of Eliza's arm. Eliza turned into her, pulled up the covers and murmured into her hair about *sleep* and *come here* and *it's okay*.

When Mia woke again, Eliza was gone.

Morning light streamed through the curtains they'd left open the night before. Mia stretched, a delicious ache in her muscles from the night before. She strained to hear the click-clack of keys, hoping Eliza was in the next room, but all she could hear was the steady crash of waves. She sat up in bed, eyeing the room for a robe of some sort. Eliza was probably in the living room and Mia would not waste another second. She was going to tell Eliza that last night had been amazing. That she'd developed feelings for her and that maybe they could keep this thing going, whatever this was, even after the week was over.

When she made her way into the living room, she discovered a carafe of coffee, a covered plate of pastries. They were *cassatelle*—pastries bursting with sweet ricotta—along with a pitcher of freshly pressed orange juice. Mia loved *cassatelle*. Had Eliza known? Maybe she saw her enjoying them the other morning, powdered sugar stuck to the tips of her fingers? She bit off the corner of the pastry and picked up a handwritten note.

> Mia,
> I got called away for an early morning meeting. I didn't want to wake you. Saved you one of those moon shaped pastries with the good cheese I know you like.
> xx, Eliza

Mia clutched the note to her chest. The tiny little x's next to Eliza's name shouldn't make Mia's heart flutter, but they certainly did. This was for the best. She really wanted to talk to Eliza, but if she didn't meet her parents for their family brunch on time, they were going to come looking for her. She had just enough time to sneak back to her room, shower and get down to the main restaurant.

Not even their strong desire to be well liked could keep the scowls from Mia's parents' faces. They stared at her pointedly as she sat down across from them and gently placed her napkin in her lap. They didn't speak as the server poured Mia a generous cup of coffee, nor while she stirred in a small bit of cream.

"Well, Mia, I hope you've had your fun." Her father brought his own coffee cup to his mouth and took a sip. "But you will end things with Eliza as soon as this week is over. We already spoke with the Richardses. They said Beth would be willing to try again, or at least be your date to some high-profile events. Beth is exactly the type of person you need by your side as you move into your new role in this family."

Mia couldn't process all the words coming out of his mouth at once. Her stomach dropped as she replayed the words, trying to make sense of them. Mia didn't know where to start.

"Beth has a girlfriend," Mia blurted out.

Her mom rolled her eyes and her father waved at the air as if to dissipate the words.

"They're not really together," her father chided. "It's just a friend who agreed to be her date to the wedding. Besides, her parents agree that our two families are better off being connected. So you'll at least appear to date Beth over the next year."

"Dad, you can't force me to fake date someone. I'm with Eliza."

The words felt true in Mia's heart and she knew it was what she wanted. She had the sudden urge to stand up and push away from the table and scour the resort, searching for her. She wanted to tell Eliza that she wanted this to be real. It was real. And after last night, after Eliza admitted she wanted her, Mia wondered if Eliza would feel the same way. Mia didn't want to date Beth. She didn't want to date anyone if it wasn't Eliza.

"Don't be ridiculous, Mia. And keep your voice down." Her father relaxed his shoulders and took another sip of coffee. He kept his eyes on her as he carefully set his cup down. A smile crept across his face. "We just want what's best for you, dear. And you will end things with

Eliza. She has a reputation for being cold and hostile. That Brewer family is known for drama. Don't get me started on the tell-all from the former VP of sales. Her father is a tyrant and she has to be just like him. Ruthless and cold. This will reflect poorly on you. On us."

"I don't care what the tabloids say about my girlfriend, Dad. She isn't like that. She's powerful and confident and I'm not breaking up with her just to create some kind of perfect family image you want." Mia felt a rush. After so many years of listening to them, she felt like she was in control of her life for the first time.

Never mind that Eliza wasn't actually her girlfriend. But didn't last night change things? She could still feel the brush of Eliza's fingertips as they pressed into her birthmark, the scar above her knee, the crease of her elbow.

A server approached with multiple offerings. There was a basket of warm *cornetti* filled with almond cream and Sicilian citrus marmalades, alongside a platter of juicy figs and peaches. A wooden board held a rustic *pane cunzatu*, topped with cherry tomatoes, olives and a drizzle of olive oil. Small bowls of creamy ricotta and golden honey sat ready for spreading. In front of her father, however, was a simple plate of scrambled eggs, just as boring as he liked it.

And pastries. The same pastries that Eliza

had left for Mia this morning. The sight of a *cassatelle* made something ache in Mia's chest. Hopefully Eliza would come back to the room and see her note, see the partially eaten pastry and know that Mia appreciated her.

She could think of nothing more in the world she wanted than to make Eliza feel half as cared for as Mia felt right now. She reached for the *cassatelle*, but her mother swatted her hand away.

"Mia, dear, have some of the fruit."

Mia's cheeks flushed with embarrassment. Her parents had always told her she could be anything she wanted to be. They doted on her when she was little. But in the past few years, she'd noticed that this love came with strings. And they didn't like when Mia tugged on them. They expected her to stay in line and project perfection. And they weren't afraid to remind her of it whenever she stepped out of line. She didn't want to argue. Not with this strange sense of shame creeping over her. And the niggling feeling that there was something else she hadn't asked about.

"You mentioned my new role in the family?" she asked, trying to keep her voice calm and even. Her parents were keeping something from her, and she didn't want to give herself completely away. If she could stay neutral, maybe they could come to some kind of agreement.

"Ah, yes." Her father grabbed the cinnamon bun she'd been eyeing and took a large bite just to spite her. He didn't even like cinnamon buns. Crusted sugar clung to the edge of his mouth and he wiped it away before continuing. "We know how much you like fundraising. Don't think we didn't know about your little stunt at the Fieldings' fundraiser. Really, Mia. Running off to support another family's efforts and trying to keep us in the dark. Did you really think that would work? You should have come to us. We would have helped. Besides, your mother and I talked it over and we agree."

He paused, relishing the moment. Mia gave a small nod.

"We will let you work with your brother, Parker, on some of our philanthropy efforts, if you agree to our terms."

Mia couldn't help but lean closer. This was it. This was what she wanted.

"Dad, this is amazing. I have ideas. I have so many ideas. I've been thinking a lot about how we can really elevate the Knowles name—make it about more than just what we have, but what we give." Excitement stirred in Mia. This was her chance. She pulled up the speech she'd been rehearsing for months. "I envision a foundation that champions causes close to our hearts—things like empowering young talent, supporting the arts or even creating sustainable opportunities in places that need it most. We could host elegant events, partner with top-tier institutions, but also keep things real by staying connected to the communities we're helping. It's about creating something meaningful, with impact and grace."

Her father held up a hand to stop her. "Okay, okay, Mia. Clearly, you've been thinking about this a lot. No need to get so excited. We're at brunch." He shoveled a bite of scrambled egg into his mouth and chewed thoughtfully. "So it's settled. You'll end things with Eliza, agree to attend some events with Beth and you can meet with Parker to share these...ideas."

When he laid it out so plainly, anger flared hot in Mia's chest. He was offering her everything she wanted. But at what cost?

"Mia dear, listen to your father." Her mother leaned in close and dropped her voice to a whisper. "Eliza might not want to even date you in a month. You would be foolish to turn down this opportunity and then lose Eliza anyway."

Her mother had a way of crushing Mia's spirit before it even had a chance to fly. She knew right where to push. Somehow, her mother knew that Mia had real feelings for Eliza, and she was determined to smother them. This was the Fieldings' fundraiser night all over again. Her mother ignoring what Mia wanted and pretending not to notice when her daughter was crushed.

Maybe her mother was right. There was no guarantee that Eliza wanted to date her after this week. And even if she did, there was no guarantee that it would last. But her dad wasn't offering her much of an opportunity. It was barely a promise. One meeting, with her own brother. But it was still more than she'd ever been given before.

"If I agree to your terms," Mia said cautiously, "what would my role be? When would I be able to get started?"

Her mother and father exchanged nervous glances. "Dear," her mother said cautiously. "It's uncouth to talk about money at brunch. Best to leave all that for later. Next week, you can meet with Parker and share some ideas. Then your father can decide what happens next."

Her father nodded once with finality and her mother leaned over to pat her hand. They still treated her like she was fifteen. And they were placating her now just as much as they did back then.

It wasn't much, but it was more than she'd heard from her parents in a long time. At least she'd been able to share some ideas. Kind of. But she wouldn't say yes, not yet. She needed to talk to Eliza.

Eliza

Eliza smiled down at the papers in front of her. She'd been doodling on the corner of her yellow notepad most of the morning. She'd just now realized it was slightly in the shape of Sicily. Or maybe Mia's birthmark. Both?

Eliza let out a little breath of laughter.

"Eliza, did you hear what I just said?" Her father let out an exasperated sigh. "Honestly, where is your head this week?"

That caught Eliza's attention. She was sitting next to her father on a Zoom call with three other board members. This was some kind of emergency meeting to prep for a merger that was still weeks away.

"I'm here," she said curtly. "I just don't understand why we are having this meeting now. Couldn't this wait until after Noah's wedding? When we are all back in New York?" She wanted to ask why her father was sitting in on the meeting at all. Normally, she handled these meetings. She'd been doing it for the past six months since she took over as CEO.

"There was an error on some documents,"

her VP of sales said as his face filled the laptop screen. "When I called you to review the changes, your phone was off. So I, um, I called Mr. Brewer to confirm."

"I see," Eliza said, narrowing her eyes at the man. They would have to have a conversation when she got back in the office. Eliza was good at her job. One missed call should not be enough to make someone call her retired father. And they all knew it. "Well, we are here now. If there is nothing else, I have a vacation to get back to."

Her father cleared his throat, but it sounded more like a growl. "You mean a girl to get back to," he said under his breath.

A shiver ran down Eliza's spine.

"Gentlemen, I will catch up with you on Monday," she said. She slammed the laptop closed without signing off or waiting for a goodbye. "Father, if you have something to say, please say it."

She expected him to back down. Usually, he was too busy to be concerned with who occupied Eliza's bed, as long as it didn't interfere with work. But apparently he didn't like what was happening.

"Since when do you let emotions get the best of you?" he said. He sounded more disappointed than angry. Which was so much worse. "You and I have been planning your future since you were a little girl. You wanted this. I built this empire for you. I don't want you to throw it all away on some relationship that won't last. Be sensible, Eliza."

She stiffened. "Father, there is nothing I take more seriously than my work. You know that. Just because I am dating Mia, it doesn't mean I can't be good at my work. She won't get in the way."

"But the dancing. The late nights."

"I am at my brother's wedding. I would do those things either way," she lied. But her father's face fell a bit. "Listen, I know you're worried I'm getting too close, getting too involved. But this is for Noah. I want to make sure he has the best wedding week possible. Part of that is attending events, playing along."

Her father nodded. "And this thing with Mia?"

"This thing with Mia is nothing. A distraction during the week. Come Monday, I will be back in the office, working harder than ever before." Her eyes stung as she said the words. But she'd get them out. She needed to convince herself as much as her father.

Mia had looked so beautiful this morning. Her hair fanned out on the pillow as she lightly snored. Eliza had lain there for a few extra minutes, memorizing the way her chest rose and fell with each breath. The way she still smelled liked citrus and something floral, even after a night of dancing and being wrapped in each other's arms. Dancing and making love. Because that's what they had done. Eliza couldn't deny it.

And now she denied the whole thing. Because she had to. People like Eliza didn't get to have happy endings. She couldn't have Mia and this empire she'd built with her father.

"Good. I don't think I need to remind you that you and I are built differently. Don't lead that girl on. I see the way she looks at you."

"I don't know what you're talking about."

Eliza surreptitiously wiped under her eyes and slid her laptop into her bag. She needed to get out of here. She needed to get back to her room. Hopefully Mia would be gone. And Eliza could take a long shower, rinse away the feel of Mia's mouth on her skin and get her head back in the game.

Her father placed a hand on her shoulder, the way he sometimes did when he dropped his guard and wanted to be sincere. "Eliza." His voice dropped to a low timbre. Eliza felt five years old. "I know this is hard. I know what it's like to choose stability and work ethic over… love. But trust me. It's for the best. For you. And for her."

"Understood," Eliza said. She pushed back

her chair and placed her bag over her shoulder. She had to get out of here. She couldn't handle her father being sincere. It was so much worse than when he was tough on her. "You have nothing to worry about."

And with that, Eliza left her father's suite and waited until she was in the elevator to let out the sob building in her throat.

CHAPTER THIRTEEN

Mia

SAND SPRAYED UP behind Mia as her feet dug into the soft area of the beach where the surf had been only an hour before. With each footfall, she replayed her parents' words in her mind. They'd let her *meet* with Parker. She could share some ideas. They were empty words with empty promises.

Even so, she'd never heard them spoken before. Her parents had never given her this much. She so desperately wanted to cling to the possibility of her dream career. But was it worth the cost of not being able to see if this thing with Eliza could really go somewhere?

Either way, Mia didn't have much of a choice. What her parents had offered her was little more than lip service. And Parker would never cross their father. She could try talking to him, but if her dad had already made up his mind, there was nothing she could do. But the idea of posing for pictures with Beth by her side made her skin crawl. She'd practically run away from brunch and threw on her running clothes. She needed an escape.

It was what she had wanted only a matter of weeks ago. To prove to Beth that she had matured, that she could handle long distance. But not like this. And not when there was *something* there with Eliza.

"Mia?" a woman's voice called out from a few paces behind her.

Her heart lurched into her throat, hoping it would be Eliza. But that was just her mind playing tricks on her. She slowed her pace and looked behind her.

A woman in her late forties pushed forward to catch up with her. Her straight brown hair was neatly pulled up in an elastic band and her leggings and tank top were a familiar running brand. She didn't have any makeup on and pulled an earbud out as she caught up to Mia. She knew this woman. It took her longer than it should have to recognize her when she wasn't in a gown or giving a speech.

"Oh. Mrs. Fielding." Mia worked to catch her breath and slowed her pace to a walk.

Mrs. Fielding smiled at her graciously. "Please. Call me Laura."

Her eyes were a clear blue and there were fine lines around her eyes. Mia had always liked Mrs. Fielding. She admired her work with her family, her dedication to funding educational programs, and now the fact that she was running without makeup and didn't seem to mind at all.

"Thanks for slowing down. I can run, but I can't talk at the same time. And I really wanted to talk to you. Eliza told me I could probably find you out here."

Mia's heart fluttered at the idea of Eliza knowing her schedule. And more so knowing she didn't have time for an early-morning run since she'd been…otherwise occupied. Or maybe she'd been watching for her from a balcony somewhere.

"Oh," Mia said, working to keep her voice even. "Is everything okay Mrs. F— Laura?"

She waved her hand at Mia and smiled. "Yes, everything is great. I've been meaning to contact you to go to lunch ever since the fundraiser, but life got so busy. When I saw you at the sunset mixer two nights ago, I knew I had to catch you before the wedding."

Nerves churned in Mia's stomach. Maybe something had happened at the fundraiser? Or maybe she was the one who told Mia's parents that she'd helped in secret. She wouldn't be mad at Mrs. Fielding. She could let that go.

Mia blew out a breath and slowed even more. "Anything. How can I help?"

Mrs. Fielding smiled at her. "I have a good feeling about you. That fundraiser was one of our biggest events ever. When I debriefed with our team, your name came up several times. According to my assistant, you're organized and have an amazing eye for pulling in donors."

A rush of pride ran through Mia when she remembered that night. She'd worked so hard. And it had paid off. The sense of accomplishment she'd felt at the end of that night was unreal. And she'd been chasing it ever since.

"Thank you," she said. "Thank you so much. It really means a lot to me."

Laura nodded. "So, I hope you don't think this is too forward, and if you're already too busy with your own family's work, I understand. But I would love to have you come on board with the Fielding Foundation—in a formal capacity. Eliza mentioned you have a master's in public administration. It wouldn't be a glamorous job, but if this is something you're wanting to continue with, we'd love to have you."

"You're...you're offering me a job?"

Laura's face fell a bit and her mouth formed a thin line. "Once again, dear, I'm not trying to take you away from your family. Especially because we would need you at our offices in Manhattan. You'd need to relocate from upstate New York. But I just knew I'd never forgive myself if I didn't ask."

Mia felt like she might float away. This was a dream and she was going to wake up any moment. She wasn't expecting this at all. And she'd gotten this offer based on her merits. Her hard work.

"That's very kind of you, but—"

"Please, dear, you don't have to answer right now. Why don't I send you over some details? Let us know next week, when we're all back on East Coast time. We are looking at a few different candidates, but like I said, I have a good feeling about you."

"This means a lot to me. Thank you for finding me and telling me."

"Don't thank me. Thank Eliza. I ran into her in the library a little bit ago. She seemed a little sad, but once we started talking about you, she perked right up."

"So Eliza mentioned me?"

"Well, I may have brought up the fundraiser. It was the last time Eliza and I had seen each other. It was a very natural conversation. I've known Eliza since she was a little girl. She is serious and dependable and goes after exactly what she wants. The other night, at the mixer, that's how she looked at you. You're very lucky."

Mia didn't know what to say. That same feeling came back over her, a sense of calm and understanding. If Mrs. Fielding could sense it, then maybe she and Eliza were on the same page.

Laura patted her on the arm and tipped her head back toward the resort. "I'm going to head back. Promise me you'll think about a position with us."

"I will. Thank you so much for the offer."

"I'll see you at the wedding."

Mia stood in the sand and watched Laura jog back toward the resort. Laura Fielding wanted her. On her own merit. In New York. But at what cost to her relationship with her parents?

And then there was what she had to say about Eliza. Mia went through the conversation in her mind again. Laura had said Eliza seemed sad. Mia reached into her shorts pocket and pulled out her phone. She sent her a quick text to Eliza asking where she could meet her.

If something had gone wrong in a meeting, there was no telling what state Eliza would be in. Mia needed to find her. She wanted to help her the same way Eliza had helped pull her out of her own intrusive thoughts.

She shoved her phone away and started a steady pace back to the resort.

Eliza

The library had been a refuge for Eliza when she first arrived at the resort. She'd turned it into a semiprivate space for a home office when she needed to get work done and required a change of scenery. And then Mia had waltzed in that second day and changed everything.

Now every trace of this library had Mia written all over it. The deep blue velvet sofa where she'd perched that first day. The brown leather book she'd held in her hands as she listened in on Eliza's call. She was everywhere.

Earlier when Laura Fielding had walked in, Eliza thought it might be Mia. She'd been ready to tell her they needed to call this off now. Her father was getting suspicious. Her mother seemed to love Mia and was probably planning to have a second daughter-in-law by this time next year. She and Mia could attend the wedding together, they would be cordial, but they couldn't *be* together again. Not like last night. Then Laura had mentioned her and Eliza couldn't help but smile.

Her phone buzzed in her pocket, but she ignored it. She was too keyed up from last night, and now this morning. She just needed five more minutes before she returned to the real world. Five more minutes in this space that reminded her of the woman she had to say goodbye to in just two days.

God, the room even smelled like Mia. Vanilla and citrus and want. Eliza closed her eyes and rubbed her temples. She needed to pull herself together. This thing with Mia had to stop.

"I thought I might find you in here," a soft voice murmured from somewhere behind her. *Mia.* It was as if she could conjure her just by thinking about her. There was a soft click of the door closing and a lock sliding into place. Or maybe it was Eliza's imagination.

Eliza huffed out a steadying breath and willed her pulse to slow. She didn't turn around; she didn't open her eyes. Maybe this was still her imagination. But then there were fingers brushing along her neck, and hands gently squeezing her shoulders.

"Are you okay?" Mia asked. She leaned down and pressed a single kiss to the top of Eliza's shoulder.

And no, she wasn't okay. But how could she tell this woman, this amazing woman, that this had to stop?

"Rough morning," she said instead. She reached up and took Mia's hands in hers, pulling her down and wrapping Mia's arms around her in a hug.

"No, don't. I just finished a run."

Mia tried to pull away, but Eliza didn't care. She pushed her chair back and took in Mia. She was in the world's tiniest running shorts and a sports bra. Her hair was pulled up in a tangled mess and she was wearing running shoes in ridiculous neon colors.

Eliza bit her lower lip.

"Please don't tell me you're into this sweaty look."

"I am not into this at all," Eliza said, pressing her lips together to hide a smile. "Come here." She pulled Mia down onto her. Mia straddled her lap and gasped.

"Eliza Brewer. We are in a very public library."

"Don't think I didn't hear you close the door."

"And locked it, too." Mia sighed and cupped Eliza's face. "You're going to have to shower again."

Eliza shrugged. "I like you like this. Stay."

In response, Mia leaned forward and pressed a chaste kiss to Eliza's mouth.

"Thank you," Mia murmured against Eliza's mouth. "For talking to Mrs. Fielding. She offered me a job."

Eliza stopped kissing. "Mia, that's amazing. Is that what you want?"

"I don't know." Mia told Eliza about her conversation with her parents. About their empty promises and thinly veiled threats.

"So they want you to be with Beth?" Eliza said, doing her best to hide her disappointment.

"I don't think they know what they want. They want to make all the decisions is all. They want positive publicity. Really, I think they just want to know they can control me. As long as it's their idea, then they're happy."

"But do you think they're right? Would Beth be a good choice for your image?"

Eliza knew Mia was going to date other people after this. She *knew* it. But the idea of approving and seeing photos of her and Beth as early as next month made her stomach turn into angry knots.

"I don't care about my image, Eliza." Mia caught Eliza's face in her hands and pressed their foreheads together. "I am done caring about what my parents think. I want to make my own choices. And if that's dating a billionaire CEO or working for another family or moving to New York, that's my choice."

Eliza felt as though the wind had been knocked from her. Eliza's heart thundered in her chest as she searched Mia's face for any sign she was joking around. Mia was imagining a future for the two of them. As if it would be the easiest thing in the world. The part they were definitely not going to talk about until they had to. Until it was time to say goodbye. Didn't she realize how impossible that would be for Eliza? She shifted in her chair and willed her voice to remain calm.

"Mia, I—"

Mia cut her words off by pressing her mouth against Eliza's again. Harder this time. When she slipped her tongue into Eliza's mouth and ran it along the edge of her tongue, all coherent thoughts fell away from Eliza's brain. She *would* remind Mia—and herself—that this thing between them was still just an arrangement. That it *had* to be just an arrangement.

But not right now.

Eliza Brewer knew when she'd lost a fight; she knew when she'd gotten the best deal and when she wouldn't be able to push anymore. And she'd definitely lost this one. She was once again powerless under Mia's touch. So she sank farther into the chair and let her fingers trail along Mia's stomach. Her fingertips ran over skin, the waistband of her shorts and down each side to her exposed upper thighs. She couldn't let herself think about tomorrow. She could only think about now.

"These shorts are killing me." Eliza grasped a handful of the thin fabric and hissed when

Mia kissed down her neck. "I can't think when you're doing that."

"Good," Mia said, her breath hot against Eliza's neck and earlobe. "I don't want you thinking. I want you touching me."

God, they were in a library. The door might be locked, but this was still a public space. This was a terrible idea. Still, her hand twitched, begging her to do as Mia asked. She should say no, but she knew if she didn't get her hands on Mia right then, she would regret it for the rest of her life.

This time was different from last night. Last night was slow, and gentle, a beginning. A conversation between their two bodies where they were teaching each other and taking their time.

But this was need and want and giving Mia relief. Eliza didn't waste time. She moved to where Mia wanted her most. This was fast and hot and Mia's eyes went wide with surprise and gratitude. Mia curved her body over Eliza's. She panted into her ear and closed her eyes and pressed their foreheads together.

"Is this okay?" Eliza asked as she moved her hand in a steady rhythm. Mia gasped and cried out and nodded against Eliza's forehead.

"Don't stop," she said hoarsely. It was practically a sob.

Eliza didn't stop.

"You're so brilliant, Mia."

Her words of praise made Mia squirm and whimper. But she needed to say them. She needed Mia to know how amazing she was. So brave and so beautiful and so, so captivating.

"I'm so proud of you for knowing what you want. For asking for it. Take everything you want from me now. Take it all. I can give you what you need."

It was on those words that Mia broke apart against Eliza's fingers. She collapsed into her arms and buried her face into Eliza's neck.

"Oh my God," she said sometime later. "I've ruined your shirt. I've ruined everything."

Eliza smirked and brushed a single tear away from Mia's face. "Maybe you can come back to my room with me and help me shower?"

A small smile creeped along the edge of Mia's mouth. "We don't have dinner for a few more hours," Mia hedged.

"Good, I intend to use them all to our advantage."

Mia stood and helped Eliza adjust her clothing as best they could.

The door clicked open. "Hello?"

"I thought you *locked* the door," Eliza hissed.

Mia shrugged looking sheepish. "I thought so, too," she whispered. "Act casual."

Cate and her entourage of bridesmaids entered the room. Mia's face turned a gorgeous crimson, highlighting the freckles on her face. Her lips were swollen and her hair was mussed. Beth narrowed her eyes and glanced from Mia to Eliza. Eliza gave a small wave, feeling a surge of confidence.

"Hi, Cate. What's up?" Mia said, her voice pitched high.

"We need to steal you away for a spa afternoon, remember? Aren't you checking the itinerary?"

"Oh, I'm so sorry." Mia fumbled for her phone. "You're right. I think I got the times mixed up."

"This was a last-minute add on the group text," Beth said. It was clear she was trying to keep her voice calm. "Maybe keep your phone on?"

"Eliza, do you want to come?" Mia turned to Eliza with a hopeful glance.

But Eliza was in desperate need of a shower and some fresh air. Now that she was coming down from the high of undoing Mia, she needed a few minutes.

"No, you go ahead. Have fun. I'll see you for dinner tonight."

Mia leaned down and gave her a soft kiss on the cheek. "Raincheck?" she murmured into

Eliza's hair. Now it was Eliza's turn to feel the familiar creep of heat on her cheeks.

She nodded once and watched Mia Knowles walk out of the library. And Eliza knew, despite what her father had told her, that she was in so much trouble. Walking away from Mia was going to be the hardest thing she would ever have to do. And maybe she didn't have to. She clung to the words her mother had said and hoped it would be enough.

Hoped *she* could be enough.

CHAPTER FOURTEEN

Mia

"Who knows, Mia, you could be next." Hannah, one of Cate's cousins, gave Mia a knowing look from across the spa. "Apparently, the Brewer siblings go from casual to serious in a heartbeat. At least Noah did. Right, Cate?"

Mia looked over at her dearest friend. A creep of pink flushed her cheeks as she pretended to be offended. "Six months isn't a whirlwind or anything. Besides, when you know, you know."

Cate looked down at her ring and smiled. When Mia and Cate were younger, Cate declared she'd never get married. And even if she did, she was keeping her name. Cate had never even dated anyone, at least not seriously, until she met Noah. Mia remembered worrying about her friend in the early months of their relationship. She and Beth were having a rough go of it, and she didn't want the same future for her best friend.

Speaking of Beth, Mia could feel the heated stare on the side of her neck and turned to find Beth, not quite glaring exactly, but not happy.

"What?" Mia asked with exasperation. She kept her voice low so no one else could hear.

"Nothing," Beth said. But she pursed her lips in a way Mia knew meant she still had more to say. So Mia raised a brow and waited her out. "It's just…you seem really happy. But I didn't hear about you and Eliza dating before this week. And when your mom talked to me this morning, she—"

Beth must have seen the look on Mia's face, and she must have looked wrecked, because Beth cut off her sentence. "You know what, never mind. We can talk about it later."

"Talk about what later?" Hannah asked. Hannah was a few years younger than Mia and Cate. She'd spent summers straggling behind the two friends, wanting to be involved in anything they were doing.

"Oh! Are we talking about Eliza?" Cate asked excitedly. The nail technician had to hold her hands in place to keep them from flailing. "Let's talk about Eliza!"

"We were *not* talking about Eliza."

"Okay, but now we are." Cate turned slightly

in her pedicure spa chair, careful not to disturb the freshly applied polish. "Have you been away together before now?"

"No, this is our first real chance to be together in person for any length of time."

"Wow," Hannah said, deadpan. "There is no way I could do long-distance like that. No thanks."

"It's not so bad." Mia shrugged. "You both just have to be willing to put in the work."

Mia stumbled over the last word, realizing too late her mistake. Beth cleared her throat and shifted in her chair, but didn't say anything.

"I bet Eliza will put in the work," Cate teased. If she knew that was Beth's reason for breaking up with Mia, she didn't let on. "I see the way the two of you interact. It's like…electricity. Not to mention what Noah walked in on."

"Oh my God, stop. Please erase that from your brain—and his."

"Come on, Mia. Give me something. We used to tell each other everything." Cate leaned in close and squeezed Mia's hand. She dropped her voice to a whisper. "What made you fall for Eliza? What do the two of you have in common besides sizzling sexual tension?"

Mia spoke without thinking. "I don't think it's what we have in common, but maybe what we bring out in each other. Eliza is bold and confident and asks for what she wants. And it makes me less afraid to do those things, too. Eliza doesn't treat me like I'm fragile. She isn't gentle with me. She knows I can handle hard things and she encourages me to pursue the things I want. And she lets me care for her. She has to be so strong, all the time, for so many reasons. But when it's just us? She lets all those walls down."

Mia stopped speaking and realized the spa had gone eerily quiet. Had the entire group just heard her? Mia's heart thundered in her chest. This whole week these feelings had been building up. She'd been collecting them like miles on her running shoes, the sole slowly wearing down in the same spots as she led up to race day. Eliza had definitely worn her down in places, made her into something softer. But also, something steady. Something she knew she could trust to get her through.

Mia wasn't planning to fall for Eliza Brewer. But when she looked at the facts, it was indisputable.

Mia didn't just want a job working with the Fielding Foundation. She didn't just want her parents' approval. She wanted it all with Eliza. And she wanted to tell her as soon as possible. Before the wedding rehearsal, if she could make it in time.

She wanted to start tomorrow as a couple for real. She wanted a real wedding date, not a fake one.

Mia stepped into the square, her strappy heels clicking against the cobblestones, a sound that seemed impossibly loud against the gentle trickle of the fountain at its center. The warm Sicilian sun kissed her bare shoulders, the thin straps of her lavender dress doing little to shield her from its touch. She glanced toward the church, its weathered stone looking impossibly quaint, as if it belonged to a postcard rather than the setting for what promised to be the wedding of the century tomorrow.

It was exactly the kind of place Mia would choose for her own wedding. Understated, steeped in history, nestled in between the old and new of the piazza. For the hundredth time, Mia marveled at how Cate and Noah had combined their styles so seamlessly. Her best friend had somehow managed to merge her jet-setting billionaire lifestyle with the quiet charm of a Sicilian village.

"Mi scusi," a no-nonsense voice called out from behind Mia. She stepped to the side, narrowly avoiding someone with a clipboard and a frown.

Mia had been so focused on the cobblestones

and the sidewalk musicians across the square, she hadn't noticed the wedding calamity happening around her. The place was swarming with florists, planners and assistants, all buzzing around to finalize details for tomorrow. Yet the church remained untouched, serene in its simplicity, like it had weathered centuries and refused to be cowed by an extravagant guest list or couture gowns.

Mia shifted the small clutch in her hand, catching her reflection in the polished glass of a café window. She looked refined, poised and, to her surprise, not entirely full of anxiety. Ever since she'd made up her mind to tell Eliza how she felt, and to make sure Eliza didn't have a way to brush it off, or skirt around it, and distract her with her mouth, she'd been a bundle of nerves.

Mia sighed, her eyes darting across the square as if conjuring the thought might summon her. She didn't see Eliza yet, but the memory of her muffled laugh against Mia's neck—low and warm, like the morning sun reflecting off the azure sea—lingered in Mia's mind.

What had started as a white lie—Mia insisting she had a date to avoid being interrogated by Cate's family and Beth especially—had turned into something far more complicated.

Fake dating wasn't supposed to feel like this.

It wasn't supposed to be catching her breath every time Eliza smiled. It wasn't supposed to be searching the room for her the moment she disappeared. It wasn't supposed to feel like this knot in her chest, part giddy excitement, part aching confusion, every time their fingers brushed.

She shook her head, trying to refocus. She would tell Eliza tonight, but not right now. Not during the wedding rehearsal. Even Mia knew that would be too much. She needed to ignore her feelings, as tangled as they were. The next few hours were about Cate and Noah. Her best friend deserved this fairy tale, and Mia would do whatever it took to help her live it, even if it meant pretending not to notice the way Eliza's touch sent a jolt of electricity up her spine.

A gust of wind stirred the bougainvillea draped over the café's wrought iron balcony, sending a few petals spiraling to the ground. Mia bent to pick one up, absently twirling it between her fingers as she walked toward the church. Her stomach fluttered at the thought of the rehearsal, of Eliza escorting her down the aisle at the end, leaning close to whisper some sly comment in her ear, her breath warm against Mia's skin.

"What are you doing out here?"

Mia looked up from the petal caught between

her fingers and saw Eliza. She was in another stunning suit. Charcoal gray with a lavender silk camisole beneath the open suit coat. Those camisoles were going to be the death of Mia.

"We match," Mia said with a giggle.

Eliza looked down and a small smile crept across her face. "You wear it better." She held out her hand to Mia. Mia took it, their fingers interlacing as she stepped to Eliza's side. "It's a good thing you're here. Noah seems off. Really nervous, I think. And no one is listening. Can you do something? Please?"

Mia hadn't realized how long she'd taken arriving at the rehearsal, but she was the last one to walk through the church doors. Inside was absolute chaos. The same woman who had blown past her moments before held a clipboard and looked frazzled. The groomsmen were scattered among the pews scrolling through their phones or chatting with each other. Beth, to her credit, was paying attention and directing her stink eye, for once, on people other than Mia.

And then there was Noah, fidgeting with the cuff of his suit sleeve and looking from one side of the room to the other. She followed his gaze and landed on Cate, who seemed to be trying to calm the group. She was answering questions, signing a paper and trying to make her way over to Noah.

"He just needs Cate," Mia said confidently. "And he needs everyone else to be quiet."

Mia tucked her fingers into her mouth and let out a wolf whistle. Highly un-heiress-like behavior. Her parents would be furious. But her parents weren't here. She could feel Eliza's heated stare as she stepped forward.

The room went quiet and Mia smiled widely. "Well, now that we're all here, why don't we get started?"

Eliza

Eliza watched in awe as Mia took action. She truly was a wonder to behold when organizing something. She handed her clutch to Eliza and began pointing and directing bridesmaids and groomsmen to the front pew on each side of the aisle.

"And who are you?" A woman with a clipboard and a severe bun glared at Mia from the edge of the church.

"Gladys, I'm so grateful you're here," Mia said soothingly. She took the nonclipboarded hand into hers and squeezed. "Since you're in charge this will no doubt be a success!"

Gladys's eyes went wide and Eliza didn't miss the small twinkle in Mia's eyes as she stood her ground. Mia had a way of putting people at ease, making sure they were acknowledged and appreciated, and she did it all without coming off as stuffy or overbearing. She was going to be brilliant at the job with the Fieldings.

As long as she took the job.

Once the group was back on track, Gladys began placing everyone for the ceremony. As each bridesmaid lined up on the left, according to Gladys's directions, the corresponding groomsmen were lined up on the right. Eliza's heart did a funny squeeze when she realized exactly what was coming.

"And Miss Mia, please stand right here." Gladys pointed to a spot on the floor at the front of the church.

Mia rose from her place on the pew, a flush of crimson running up one side of her neck. Eliza wanted to brush her fingertips against it and see if she could make Mia shiver.

Gladys looked to the bench and frowned when she realized there were no groomsmen left to place at the front of the line.

"It's Eliza," Mia said gently, never taking her eyes off Eliza.

"Excuse me?"

"Eliza. She's Noah's best woman. She stands across from me."

"Oh, yes, of course."

Eliza was buzzing with nerves. It was just a

rehearsal, for goodness' sake. If she couldn't handle this, what was she going to do tomorrow? But Mia looked stunning, and Eliza wasn't sure how she should be expected to stand across from her and not kiss her. Not want to hold her hand. Not want to promise her the entire world.

When Eliza had been placed in her spot, she looked up to find Mia still staring at her. Mia's eyes were round, and she bit the edge of her lip. "Hi," she mouthed.

Eliza felt her gaze from the top of her head to the tip of her toes.

"Well, there's something you won't see again."

Eliza tried to ignore her father's voice, but he wasn't exactly trying to be quiet. He sat in the second pew, several feet away from Eliza's mother and her new husband. He was grumbling to one of Eliza's uncles.

"What?" Uncle Jonas asked. Jonas was one of Eliza's favorite uncles. He kept his head shaved close and his goatee full and always had sweets in his desk. Sometimes Eliza still sneaked in and grabbed lemon drops from the top left drawer.

"Eliza at the altar."

She saw her dad gesture toward her out of the corner of her eye. Thankfully, Mia was distracted, listening intently while Gladys moved their hands and demonstrated for Noah and Cate the directions they should face for each portion of the ceremony.

"She doesn't have time for dating."

"Isn't she dating the woman across from her?" Her uncle seemed confused.

Just as confused as Eliza. She wanted to drop her hands and walk over to her dad and demand that he stop talking about her life as if he made all the decisions.

"For now." Her father's words seemed so final. "But soon enough, the hours will get to that girl. Eliza will come home one time too late. Or forget her birthday. Miss a dinner. That poor girl will resent Eliza and it will end. It always ends."

"That's a pretty terrible way of looking at love." Jonas rubbed at his chin. "I don't know, they look pretty happy."

Her father harrumphed and crossed his arms across his chest. Eliza felt the hot sting of her eyes burning and blinked back angry tears.

"Eliza is built of something different. Like me. That's why I chose her over Noah. She has what it takes. She can do this. The company is going places with her."

Eliza took a shuddering breath and worked to control her emotions. Her father was talking low and no one else seemed to be paying attention. Mia was absorbed in the directions of the wedding planner. Eliza let out one more slow breath in relief. She didn't want her to know any of this. Dread, guilt and shame spiraled down her throat, burying themselves in her stomach.

"And if she doesn't? What if she stays with Mia? It's Mia, right?"

"She won't. I've seen the way Eliza looks at that girl. She loves her. Too much to give her the same life I had with her mother. A relationship that ends in pain and unresolved anger. Eliza is too smart to do that to someone."

Eliza's head snapped toward her father, but he was already looking at her. Their eyes connected and he stared at her before saying, "Our legacy is too important. She'll make the right choice."

Eliza couldn't breathe. Her father's words had punched her in the stomach and she gasped. He *knew*. He knew she'd been listening this whole time. Her father put business above everything else. And he assumed she would do the same. He assumed she'd hurt Mia like he'd hurt Eliza's mother. And what if he was right?

She tried to keep her focus on Mia. Her soft curls and determined smile lit up the chapel. But the walls felt like they were closing in. Her father's words echoed in her ears. How long until she hurt Mia?

"Okay. Well done, everyone. We'll save the kissing for tomorrow." Gladys clasped her hands together with finality, but Eliza wasn't sure what had just happened. "Cate and Noah, please proceed down the aisle. Mia and Eliza, you're next."

Gladys's words hung in the air. Mia stepped forward and squeezed Eliza's fingers. Eliza stared down at their joined hands, wishing she knew what she was supposed to do.

"I'm sorry, what?"

"You and Mia. You can exit down the aisle." She gestured to Noah and Cate waiting at the back of the church.

Eliza dropped Mia's hands and backed up. "Oh yes. Yes, of course." But her feet didn't stop moving. "Sorry, I'll be right back. Just need some air."

And before anyone could ask questions, Eliza walked down the aisle, alone, and out the doors of the church into the afternoon sun.

CHAPTER FIFTEEN

Mia

BY THE TIME Mia made it out the door to check on Eliza, she'd disappeared down one of the side streets. Mia had walked the cobblestone path around the fountain, calling out her name before finally trying Eliza's phone.

After two rings, she was sent to voicemail. Eliza needed space. That must be what this was. Her baby brother was getting married and she needed a moment. And so that's what Mia gave her for the rest of the afternoon.

As she dressed for the rehearsal dinner that night, Mia reflected on how much had changed since she'd first arrived at La Piccola Barca. This resort, once a shell of a hotel, was now a bustling and vibrant destination, complete with memories to last a lifetime for Mia.

Mia checked the intricate wooden box for the wedding itinerary. She added the bougainvillea petal she'd caught in her fingers outside the café to the box, along with other mementos she'd hidden away that week. A matchbook from the club where she and Eliza had first kissed, a small scoop of sand in a jar from the day she and Eliza had escaped on the paddleboard to the secluded lagoon, and finally a small black button that had come off of Eliza's tuxedo coat the night they'd first agreed to this ridiculous arrangement. Mia picked up the button and rolled her eyes at herself. *Who keeps the button from a stranger's shirt?* Maybe she knew, even then, that this would turn into something.

Mia pocketed the button for good luck and then shut the box and placed it back on the nightstand in her room before heading to the rehearsal dinner.

The terrace had been utterly transformed, reborn as a lush Sicilian orchard that seemed to have sprung straight from a fairy tale. Towering olive trees in ornate, hand-painted ceramic pots stood sentinel along the balcony of the terrace, their gnarled branches twisted with age and wisdom, their silvery-green leaves catching the glow of string lights above. The deep blue ocean crashed behind the trees.

Everywhere Mia looked, lemon trees stood proudly in large clay pots, their vibrant yellow fruit gleaming like jewels under a canopy of twinkling lights. The trees framed the terrace, their glossy leaves catching the warm glow of hanging lanterns and strings of fairy lights, which seemed to merge with the stars overhead. Tables were nestled among the trees, draped in creamy linens and adorned with clusters of fresh lemons, sprigs of thyme and delicate white blossoms spilling from more of the cobalt blue pottery. The air shimmered with the bright, intoxicating scent of citrus mingled with a hint of thyme and the salty tang of the nearby sea.

She spotted Eliza across the terrace. She was always spotting Eliza across the terrace. Mia waved, feeling ridiculously smitten, and not caring one bit. Eliza nodded back before downing the remains of her champagne glass and heading toward Mia. Her stomach flipped with anticipation as Eliza drew closer.

"All right, everyone, let's all take a seat."

Mia jumped at the boom in Mr. Brewer's voice. It was as if he was trying to keep Mia and Eliza apart. Or at least keep them from talking. Mia found her spot, to the right of Cate at the longest table. Eliza took her own spot, two seats down. All through dinner, Mia tried to make conversation with Eliza, but Eliza seemed to brush her off.

"So, when do you head back?" Noah asked Eliza.

"Tomorrow night, as soon as the reception is over." Eliza's words were like ice over Mia. Tomorrow night?

"Oh, you'll miss the Sunday brunch. Don't go so soon," Cate said. "Mia, are you leaving that soon, too?"

Mia didn't have words. She blinked at them all. "Oh," she said when she realized they were all expecting a response. "I don't... I don't know."

Eliza widened her eyes at Mia in disbelief. They seemed to say *of course you aren't coming back with me.* It made Mia feel rotten.

"Well, when we get back from our honeymoon, we'll have to all get together. Mia, how often are you in New York?"

Never. But no, not never. She had a potential job. With the Fieldings. In New York. "Actually, I think I will be in more often. Laura Fielding offered me a job. And I promised to at least meet with her. If it goes well, I could be in New York quite a bit."

Cate squealed and leaned over, wrapping Mia in a hug. At least one person at the table was happy about the news. Eliza picked up her glass and took a long sip of something warm and brown.

"Okay, so we will all plan something then—

it's settled." Noah squeezed Eliza's hand and Eliza winced.

"I'm sure Mia will be busy with work." Eliza shrugged. "I will be, too. I have a tight schedule once I'm back. And I need to hire a new editor for our sightings page."

"Oh, I heard about that." Noah nodded. "Good for you."

"What are you talking about?" Cate asked.

"I'll be right back," Eliza said. She pushed back her chair and rushed away.

"That was weird. She's been weird since the rehearsal. Anyway, she fired someone for posting those pictures of her and Mia without permission. In fact, she's banned anyone from posting Mia's photograph until further notice."

"Oh, that's so romantic."

"Yeah, Dad was mad. But he's not the one in charge anymore. Which…also makes him mad."

Mia couldn't believe what she was hearing. Not only did Eliza protect her. But she stood up to her father to do it. She pushed back her own chair and blurted out, "I need to go."

She wasn't sure which way Eliza had run off to. But she took a chance and headed to the one spot, beyond the assembled grove of trees, where she thought Eliza might be hiding.

The night had turned cold. Mia wrapped her

arms around her shoulders as she stepped onto the empty terrace.

"Eliza?" she called out.

It was dark on the terrace; this area was not meant for guests. But Mia would know the curvy silhouette of Eliza anywhere. She looked especially lovely in the shadowed moonlight, even if she was slumping against the railing.

"I guess you *do* make it a habit of barging into people's private spaces."

A shiver went down Mia's spine at the words. She would know that smooth, low voice anywhere.

"This is twice in one week, Knowles."

Eliza stepped into the light.

"You won't let anyone take pictures of me?"

Eliza shrugged. "It was nothing. The other ones never should have been published."

Eliza barely got the words out before Mia's mouth was on hers. She needed Eliza to know how much this meant to her, how much *she* meant to her. Eliza stiffened beneath Mia's touch, but soon became pliant. Mia took Eliza's bottom lip into her mouth and sucked before Eliza finally gave in and kissed her back.

"No one has ever done something like that for me before." Mia cupped Eliza's face in her hands and searched Eliza's eyes for understanding. "That must have cost your magazine a fortune."

"I don't care about the money, Mia. No one should get to decide how you appear in the media except for you. Not me, not your parents. You."

Eliza cupped Mia's cheeks with her hands and Mia leaned in to the caress. Eliza pulled Mia's hands down and clasped them in hers. Mia curled her fingers around Eliza's and looked into Eliza's eyes.

"I don't want this to end," Mia said. It was a whisper. A plea. Even as she spoke it, she saw Eliza's face change.

"Mia, I—"

"I know you're busy with work. I know you have an entire life. But there's something here. I've never felt this way about anyone before. And I know it's only been a week, but I am falling for you, Eliza Brewer. Somewhere between our ridiculous pact, to the gondola ride, to that kiss on the dance floor. I fell for you."

Eliza shook her head. But Mia wasn't sure if it was a no, or if she couldn't believe what Mia was saying. So she continued.

"I love that you're brave and strong, but you get soft for me. I love taking care of you, even when you don't need it. And I don't want this to end. I want to see where this goes."

Mia's heart was pounding, her pulse thrumming in her ears as the words left her lips. But now, as she watched Eliza's expression, the light of the lanterns flickering in her conflicted eyes, Mia felt her chest tighten with the first crack of doubt.

"Eliza," she said again, her voice quieter now, almost pleading. "You feel the same way. I know you do. You told me you wanted this last night outside the restaurant. Why can't we make this real? Tell me you want to try."

Eliza looked away, her jaw tightening as she gripped the stem of her champagne flute. "Mia…" she began, but her voice faltered. She exhaled sharply, then forced herself to turn back, meeting Mia's gaze with eyes filled with something raw, something almost like regret. "You don't understand. This—what we've had here—it's been perfect, more than I ever expected. But it's not my real life."

Mia stared at her, confusion blooming into disbelief. "What do you mean it's not your real life? It doesn't have to end. We can—"

"No." Eliza cut her off, her voice trembling even as she tried to steady it. "You don't get it. My father built everything we have, Mia. He worked tirelessly to give Noah, and me, a future. And it broke him and my mother. It broke them and she never recovered. This is his legacy. He expects me to do the same. And I can't let him down. I won't. I don't have time for anything else. He's hard on me because he has to be, and I've learned to be just as hard on myself. I don't have time for you. My work...it's my whole life. It has to be."

Mia felt the weight of the words crash over her, but she couldn't stop herself. "It doesn't have to be," she whispered, stepping closer, her hands reaching out but hesitating just shy of touching Eliza. "You don't have to do it all on your own. You can let someone in. Let me in."

Eliza didn't answer. She didn't have to. The look in her eyes said everything.

"So this was all pretend for you?"

"Don't say that," Eliza practically growled. "I told you. I told you what I can give. What I'm capable of. You don't want me. Don't you see? I don't get happy endings. I don't get the girl. I have work, and I have my family. I have obligations. They need me to make sure everything stays on track."

"I can't believe this," Mia said. Mostly to herself. "Eliza, you can have this. We can figure it out. You're being selfish." Mia felt anger and frustration building in her, causing her shoulders to tense and her eyes to brim with tears. "So you do want this. But you're still saying no. We could at least try, Eliza. You keep telling me to be brave. To stand up to my parents. But what about you? Isn't this worth the risk? Or are you too scared to be happy?"

Eliza scoffed. "Happy? You are the *one* thing I want, Mia. Being with you is the *only* thing I want. But I can't have that. I can't have that and not hurt you. You're going to resent me. But don't for one second think I'm being selfish. I am only thinking of you. I am going to break your heart, Mia."

The words crashed over Mia and she practically swayed with the impact. Eliza thought she was doing this to protect her. Eliza slumped, the fight leaving her, and she reached for Mia. But Mia snatched her hands away. She couldn't feel Eliza's hands on her again, knowing Eliza wouldn't choose her.

"Yeah," Mia said softly. She wiped at another tear, desperate to maintain her composure until she could get back to her room. "I'll see you tomorrow, okay? I'll be the perfect date. No one will know that none of this was real. And then I'll leave you alone."

Eliza

Eliza shut her eyes and leaned over the balcony. She couldn't bear to watch Mia walk away. There was a soft clink on the edge of the balcony next to her, and then she listened to Mia's retreating footsteps.

Eliza looked down and saw one shiny black button gleaming in the moonlight. She recognized it immediately. The button Mia had accidentally ripped off her tuxedo jacket with her bracelet, their night first night here.

She'd kept it.

Eliza let out one quiet sob before picking up the button and shoving it into her coat pocket. This was for the best. Her father had been right. Eliza didn't deserve Mia. She couldn't make her happy. It was better to break her heart a little now, when it was just a hairline fracture, than to wait and break it completely. Mia would come back from this. Eliza knew she would.

Eliza wiped her eyes, straightened her coat and returned to the party. The band was in full swing, and Noah and his groomsmen had started some kind of impromptu dance party.

"Eliza, do you mind getting this guy back to his room?" Cate said, pushing Noah toward her. "I'd take him, but we aren't supposed to see each other until tomorrow. I'm staying with Beth tonight."

"Of course," Eliza said. "I've got him."

"Why aren't you with Mia?" he asked, a lilt to his words. "I like her." He hiccupped and Eliza rolled her eyes, hiding her pain.

"Of course you do. Come on."

Eliza was several years older than her brother and had never had the pleasure of escorting a drunken version of him home. Noah was a sweet drunk. He hugged everyone and everything he said sounded like a song.

"Can you believe I'm getting married tomorrow?" His eyes were wide and his voice was filled with wonder.

"Yes, I can," Eliza murmured. "We've been counting down to it all week." She helped him down the hall and grabbed the room card from his breast pocket. She swiped them into his suite and deposited him on the couch.

"You stay here. I'm going to find you some headache medicine." Eliza did what she did best. She went into fixing mode. She fetched a glass from the counter and filled it with water before locating the pills. "Here. Drink."

He dutifully drank down the pills and handed her the glass. "I'm so happy, Eliza. So, so happy."

She sat down next to him and patted his knee. "I know you are, baby brother. Cate is pretty amazing."

"No."

"No?"

"Wait. No. She is. But I mean for you. Mia is the best. And you are the best. And now the two bests can be happy together. I've never seen you like this, sis."

"Okay, I think you're really drunk."

"Nope. I speak the truth. You two are the real deal."

"Noah, we can't be. Mia and I aren't— We aren't that serious." Eliza's chest ached as she said the words. She wanted to tell her brother everything. She probably could and he wouldn't remember tomorrow. But she'd made a promise to Mia. "I don't want us to end up like Mom and Dad. I need to focus on work."

"Pfft." He waved his hand in the air as if to bat away the words she was saying. Eliza bent down and removed his shoes. He stared at them in wonder and wiggled his toes. "Mom and Dad broke up because of Mom and Dad."

"Come on, into bed with you," Eliza stood and grabbed Noah's hands, but he tugged her back down onto the couch.

"Wait, Eliza. Listen. Mom didn't leave Dad because of work. I mean, yes, that's what they fought about a lot. But work was something they fought about because it was easier to pin her anger there than on the bigger, harder to identify, things. They weren't right for each other. Maybe they never were."

Eliza felt the hot sting of tears at the edge of her eyes. She blinked back the tears, trying to keep them at bay. "It doesn't matter," Eliza sighed. "I'm no good at the girlfriend stuff. The partner stuff. She's going to give up on me eventually."

"You are *the best* at it, Eliza. Cate said she's never seen Mia so happy. And she's finally standing up to her parents? That's huge. And I think it has something to do with you."

"What?"

Eliza turned to her brother, who now had his head back on the couch. His eyes were closed and his breathing was slowing. "Hmm?" he said, only half there.

"Noah?"

"Love you, too," he mumbled. He was definitely asleep. But his words stuck in Eliza's chest.

Mia was happy. And Noah thought it had something to do with Eliza. A zip of pleasure, of hope, coursed through her, pulsing and bright, settling in her chest.

She grabbed a pillow and blanket from his bed, knowing there was no way she could move her brother from the couch now that he was snoring. She tucked him in like she'd done so many times when they were little and kissed the top of his head.

When Eliza returned to her suite, she was overwhelmed with the absolute emptiness of it. She'd spent two nights with Mia in that bed. Two glorious and wonderful nights. The sheets still smelled like her. Citrus and flowers.

Eliza had never felt so alone.

Eliza did not want to admit it, but her brother might be right. She thought about the look in Mia's eyes. The absolute anger and hurt when Eliza put an end to things tonight. No, this was for the best. She needed to protect Mia, even if it meant breaking her own heart in the process.

Eliza closed her eyes, but sleep didn't come. She walked over to the windows and peered out, hoping to see Mia running along the beach. Some kind of sign that she'd made a mistake. But the beach was silent and still. The only movement was the steady lap of waves on the shore and the full moon casting light across the sea.

CHAPTER SIXTEEN

Mia

THE CHURCH WAS dripping in white flowers, lush and opulent. Every surface had been touched since they'd left the night before. Mia looked out the window from the side of the church and to the fountain in the middle of the square. Less than a day before she'd stood there with Eliza, holding hands in the sunlight and whispering to each other.

And now it was all washed away. Mia knew Eliza had feelings for her. She knew it in the way Eliza looked at her and the way she held her. But if Eliza wasn't ready to admit those feelings, if she wasn't ready to be fully present, then Mia had no choice.

"You know—" A voice interrupted Mia's thoughts and she jumped, letting the thin curtain drop from her fingers. "I didn't break up with you because of the long distance."

Mia spun to find Beth standing in front of her. "But that's what you said…"

"Of course that's what I said." Beth rolled her eyes. Like she wasn't almost thirty. "You're an heiress. The sweetheart of the Knowles empire. The life of the party. One look from you would make anyone feel like the luckiest person on earth."

Beth fidgeted with the edge of her dress and cleared her throat. "But I knew when you looked at me, you didn't feel the same way." Mia wanted to protest but Beth held up her hand.

"It's okay. And I'm sorry I wasn't honest with you from the beginning. But Mia, look at you now. You did so much to help Cate and Noah this week. Your organization, your attention to detail, your ability to somehow convince Eliza Brewer that it's okay to have fun."

Mia's eyes pricked at the sound of Eliza's name. She sniffed and wiped away a tear. "Well, I don't know about that," she said softly.

Beth offered a sad smile. "Look, I don't know what's going on between the two of you. And I don't know why your parents are trying to interfere. But I do know that you've seemed happier this week than I've ever seen you before. And I think it had something to do with Eliza, but I think it might also have something to do with *you*. Something turned on in you this week,

Mia. And I hope you nurture whatever it is. I hope you find what you're looking for. And I hope, in some form, we can be friends."

Mia nodded and Beth reached out and squeezed her forearm.

"I'd really like that," Mia said.

Beth didn't have to say any of this, but Mia knew she was right. Even if things hadn't worked out with Eliza, she was different as a result. She was going to meet with Laura Fielding. She was going to take the job. She was probably going to move to Manhattan.

"And I hope you and Eliza are really happy together. I'm rooting for you. No matter what your parents say."

"Wow, Beth. I… I don't know what to say."

"Ladies, it's time. You need to line up." Gladys wielded her clipboard like a sword, and Mia and Beth giggled before falling in line, the last two before Cate.

Beth swatted her words away. "It's fine. Let's get my sister through this wedding, then you can thank me."

They filed into the late-afternoon sun of the courtyard and found Noah's wedding party waiting for them. Her heart clenched as she remembered who she was paired with to walk down the aisle.

Eliza looked gorgeous. She wore a fitted

black tuxedo, a strip of black silk running down her leg. It hugged every curve, but the way Eliza brought it to life with her confidence was truly what made her stand out. Her black heels made her a few inches taller than Mia.

"You look beautiful," Eliza said as Mia approached.

Mia's heart clenched. Right. They were still pretending. Putting on a show for everyone else. Mia blinked, the afternoon sun stinging her eyes, and she nodded.

"Right. So do you."

Eliza frowned. "Listen, Mia. About last night—"

"No." Mia shook her head. "Not here. Not right now. I can't talk to you and also make it through this wedding. So please, just stop."

To her credit, Eliza pressed her lips together and nodded once.

"Ladies, over here, please." Gladys motioned for Mia to join the end of the line.

Eliza held out her arm and Mia slipped hers through it. She was glad she could blame the sting in her eyes on the wedding itself. She clutched her bouquet and steeled herself for the ceremony.

"Here." Eliza pressed something into Mia's free hand. A white handkerchief with a trail of bougainvillea embroidered in one corner. Mia dabbed at her eyes and tried to return it.

"No, you keep it," Eliza insisted. "I'm sorry I can't give you everything. I can't give you what you deserve. You can at least keep my handkerchief."

"I don't want everything, Eliza." Mia would not cry. They were next to walk down the aisle. If Mia didn't say this now, she never would. So even though her voice shook, she said, "I want *you*. I want you to *try*. To take a chance, even though you're scared."

But Eliza didn't have a chance to respond. The doors to the church opened for them and everyone watched as Eliza walked Mia down the aisle.

Eliza

Cate and Noah opted for traditional vows and a simple ceremony inside the stone chapel, which meant Eliza only had to make it through about twenty minutes of awkwardness before she could escape to relative obscurity at the reception. Eliza tried to keep her eyes focused on her brother, but it was too easy to look up and see Mia's wide green eyes staring at her from across the aisle.

She was radiant in the stunning black dress.

Eliza had assumed she'd be in lavender, or sage, or some other typical color for a bridesmaid. But all the bridesmaids wore simple black dresses.

Every time Mia dabbed at her eyes with that stupid handkerchief, Eliza's heart cracked open a little more. She knew Mia deserved better than her. But maybe she also deserved better than what she was allowing for herself.

Eliza looked out into the crowd. At her father sitting in the front row. And her mother sitting next to him, her now-husband handing her a kerchief to wipe away a stray tear. Her mother smiled at her and nodded.

Eliza was scared. She was so, so scared. But when she thought about who she wanted to be a year from now, ten years from now, at the end of her life, she knew she wanted more for herself than a pile of paperwork and a legacy for one.

When Eliza laid it out like this, the answer was so simple. She looked at her mother, at her baby brother, promising to love and cherish Cate. Not promising it would be perfect, or that they would never have to compromise, but promising to love her anyway, even if they didn't know the future.

"And now, the rings." The minister looked to Noah and he turned to his sister.

She reached into her jacket pocket and produced the two platinum bands. As she pressed them into his palm, he squeezed her hand back and mouthed, "I love you."

And then seconds later, Noah and Cate were kissing and the church was applauding and they were all racing back down the aisle.

"I have a surprise for us," Noah yelled above the applause as the wedding party danced into the courtyard outside the church. Just then, the loud sound of chopper blades filled the air and a wicked smile spread across Noah's face. "Even you, Eliza. Please?"

Dread pooled in Eliza's stomach. Noah had always been the daredevil. The one who leaped first and only then made sure he had the parachute. It often worked out for him. He took chances; he took risks. And Eliza was there to catch him if he fell. Not the other way around.

There was no way she was getting on a helicopter. This was worse than the gondola. At least then she was over land.

"Noah! This is amazing," Mia yelled. Her eyes connected with Eliza's for a moment before they moved on to Cate. "I better get one of those microphone things."

Eliza looked over at Mia. She wanted to talk to her; she wanted to get her alone. She was absolutely stunning in that dress. But perhaps the most gorgeous thing about Mia was her confidence. She was so certain about what she wanted. And Eliza was a coward.

"Come on," Cate said as she removed her veil and handed it to the wedding planner. "Down to the docks."

The bridal party took off running. It was the kind of scene that only Cate and Noah could make in the tiny town square. And Eliza, rooted to the spot with fear, didn't follow after. She couldn't do it. She couldn't get on a helicopter. It was too much.

The people on the streets stopped and cheered and clapped for them as they went. Mia trailed behind them, with Beth by her side. It was the exact image Eliza had been terrified of seeing. And she hated it.

She felt a hand on her arm and turned to find her mother.

"I know you're scared," her mother said, "but sometimes we have to do things that scare us."

"Mom, I can't. I could plummet to my death. What if we crash?"

"Oh, I wasn't talking about the helicopter, dear." Her mom gave her a knowing smile. "Is she worth it? Is she worth being a little scared?"

Eliza's heart thundered in her chest. And then, before she could talk herself out of it, she started running. She lost sight of Mia, but followed the sound of cheers and clapping from the crowds. The cobblestone road was tricky with her heels, so Eliza kicked them off and prayed she wouldn't step on a rock.

By the time she reached the helicopters at the dock, the rest of the wedding party had already boarded. She wasn't even sure which helicopter Mia would be in. She spotted Cate's white dress from one window and took a chance.

The pilot waved her in and she leaped into the helicopter. Her heart was pounding, her mind was racing and she was more scared than she'd ever been in her entire life. But there was Mia Knowles, complete shock on her face, looking gorgeous.

"What are you doing?" she mouthed, her eyes wide and nervous.

"I'm telling you I'm in," Eliza practically yelled. It was so loud in this helicopter, she could barely hear her own voice.

"What?" Mia asked.

Cate handed headphones to each of them and pointed at their ears. Eliza obliged, tucking the headphones onto Mia's head before adding them to her own. She felt ridiculous, but at least she could hear Mia now.

"I'm in. With you. I want this. I'm not scared anymore." She cupped Mia's face with her hands and leaned in close. "I mean, I am scared. I'm terrified. But I want to do it anyway. With you."

She didn't care if Cate and Noah could hear her, never mind the pilot. Eliza didn't care if the entire island heard her. She wanted Mia to know that she was ready to be brave.

Eliza crashed her mouth into Mia's. Mia threw her arms around Eliza and Eliza leaned in and kissed her with passion. It was awkward. Eliza had to move the microphone out of the way. Mia was laughing and Eliza felt it against her neck.

She was scared. Terrified. But with Mia next to her, she could do this.

"And I don't care if we have to do long-distance and I don't care if it will be hard. I want to *try*. With you."

"I'm moving to Manhattan," Mia blurted out. "I'm taking the job with the Fieldings. Apparently, we are both doing things we're scared of."

Mia let out a little yelp when Eliza crashed her mouth into Mia's again. She tried to press all her emotions into her kiss. She wanted Mia to know what was in her heart. She wanted to make sure she knew all the things Eliza couldn't say out loud when the helicopter was roaring and her pulse was racing and her heart felt like it was going to beat out of her chest.

"Ma'am, I'm going to need you to buckle up." The pilot leaned back in his seat and pointed at the harness.

Eliza swallowed the lump in her throat and looked from Mia to Cate to her brother. And then she strapped herself in to this death contraption.

Her brother whooped and Cate laughed and Mia leaned over to kiss her again.

They were all given directions through their headphones with mouthpieces and Eliza shut her eyes tight and she squeezed Mia's hand as the helicopter took flight, the pressure of the ascent thrusting her back in her chair.

"Eliza, open your eyes," Mia's voice crackled in her ears. Eliza shook her head. "Babe, please. You don't want to miss this."

Mia squeezed her hand before bringing it to her mouth and kissing her knuckles. Eliza cracked open one eye and peeked at Mia. She was staring back at her.

"Eliza, look. It's so beautiful." Mia pointed somewhere out the window, but all Eliza could see was the absolute joy and wonder on Mia's face.

"Yes," Eliza agreed. "It really is."

CHAPTER SEVENTEEN

Eliza

ONCE THE HELICOPTERS LANDED, guests greeted the wedding party in the open-air ballroom. Eliza didn't regret jumping into the helicopter, but she was grateful to have her feet back on the ground and Mia still in her arms.

An exclusive restored building high above the Sicilian coastline housed the reception; the building blended old-world charm and modern opulence. The Mediterranean stretched endlessly below, its deep cerulean waters reflecting the warm glow of the golden hour. Thousands of flowers—roses, peonies and orchids—cascaded from towering arrangements at the reception, their abundance entwining pillars and spilling over tables draped in shimmering silk. Candles of every size flickered from gilded candelabras and glass votives, their warm light mingling with the soft glow of fairy lights strung in sweeping arcs across the ceiling.

The open balcony, framed by ornate railings wrapped in garlands of jasmine, overlooked the ocean as waves lapped against the cliffs below. The air was heavy with the scent of blooms and the sea, while the gentle strains of a live orchestra set an enchanting rhythm for the evening.

But Eliza wasn't going to remember any of it. How could she, when Mia was the brightest thing in the room? They moved together across the glowing mosaic-tiled dance floor, the soft candlelight catching the intricate beadwork of Mia's gown and making it shimmer like a thousand tiny stars.

Hundreds of impeccably dressed guests milled around them. Yet to Eliza, the crowd was little more than a blur, the lavish decor a distant hum. Every petal, every flicker of light, every note of music seemed to exist only as a frame for Mia.

Mia was gorgeous like this. She was always gorgeous, always had been, but her gown looked like the night sky as she swayed in Eliza's arms.

"Mind if I borrow my daughter?"

Eliza didn't miss the way Mia's eyes went wide as Eliza's father approached.

"Dad, can we talk later? I'm kind of in the middle of dancing with my girlfriend."

"I don't want to talk. I was hoping we could—" his eyes darted around the room, no doubt noticing he was making a scene "—dance?"

Eliza looked to Mia, and although fear and worry and anxiety snaked up the back of her neck, Mia gave a small nod.

"I'll be over on the balcony if you need me." She kissed Eliza on the cheek and then she was gone.

Eliza and her father fumbled as they joined hands and drifted back and forth on the dance floor.

"Girlfriend, huh?" Her father raised a brow in question.

Eliza huffed. She didn't want to do this. Not now, not at her brother's wedding reception, but she would. "Yes, Dad, my girlfriend. I… I'm serious about her. And she is going to be in my life, whether you like it or not."

Her dad didn't respond for a long time. He was an impeccable dancer. It was a shame he rarely made use of the skill.

"Then I guess I'd better meet her. Officially. Will you two join me for brunch once we're back in New York? I'd like a chance to make a, um, better impression than I've done so far this week."

"Brunch? At a restaurant?"

"Yes."

"Not a working brunch."

Her father let out a short laugh. "Not for work. I'd like to take you out. With your girlfriend. As my daughter."

"Dad, I'd... I'd really like that." She wasn't sure if she believed him, but maybe he was trying. "Did Mom put you up to this?"

"She may have suggested the brunch part. But you put me up to this. You took charge and took a stand—against me—after I approved those photos. Let's just say I might be having a hard time letting go. But I was wrong. And I'm sorry. You've done an impressive job as CEO. You're going to do things I never could. And I know... I know I need to let you do them your way."

"One brunch," Eliza agreed. "And I'm removing your work email account. You won't have access to mine anymore either. You overstepped. And I need to know that won't happen again."

She expected her father to chastise her. Or perhaps make another comment about how maybe she wasn't ready to fully take over. But instead, his eyes glimmered with something close to respect.

"Agreed," he said.

The song ended and Eliza pulled her hand away. "Now, if you'll excuse me, I need to find my girlfriend."

Mia

The fiery pink-and-orange sunset had just dipped into the sea when Mia felt a warm hand on her waist. She didn't have to turn around to recognize the firm yet gentle grip. Her body flushed and her heart raced in a way that only Eliza could elicit.

Eliza, who had somehow fallen for her as well. She'd braved a helicopter for Mia, but she'd braved so much more than that. She'd told her she wanted to try. Eliza had squeezed her eyes shut and wouldn't look down, her pulse thundering under Mia's fingertips, but she'd done it.

"How did it go?" Mia asked.

"Good. He wants to meet you. Properly."

"Sounds…scary."

"Maybe. Probably. But you'll be fine. You're brave."

"So are you," she murmured as she played with the lapels on Eliza's suit coat. "What next? Sky diving? Bungee jumping?"

Eliza huffed, and Mia felt it on the top of her hair. "I don't think so, love. Please tell me that's not a deal breaker."

"Don't worry, you're safe with me," Mia mused.

"I know," Eliza said.

Mia placed her fingertips over Eliza's heart

and drummed the beat of the next song playing in the distance. She could get used to this. Eliza under her fingertips, the world fading away around them.

"When I get back to New York things are going to be busy for a while. But I want to make time. I'm going to make time. For this. For us."

Mia's heart squeezed at the sincerity in Eliza's voice. She was under no false pretenses that Eliza was going to stop working as hard or as much as she always had, but she had plans, too. And if the email from the Fielding Foundation this morning was any indication, she'd be just as busy in New York.

"Actually," Mia said, "I'll be in Manhattan next week for a meeting with the Fieldings. Maybe we can start there."

Eliza's eyes went wide with amusement. "Mia, that's amazing. And so fast. Are you sure? Your parents—"

Eliza's eyes flashed with excitement and worry, creating a small furrow between her brows. And while Mia appreciated her protective side coming out, it wasn't necessary.

"Hey." Mia cupped Eliza's face and drew her close. As the song faded, she whispered, "We can deal with my parents later. I *will* deal with my parents later. But for now, can we just enjoy this?"

Eliza pulled Mia close and whispered into

her hair, "Of course. I can't think of anything I want to do more than hold you close right now." She kissed her hair, then her temple, and finally her lips, which were quirked into a small smile.

Mia squeezed Eliza at the waist and Eliza's brain went fuzzy with warmth and happiness—and something else, too. Eliza led her out to the dance floor and pulled Mia close. Eliza inhaled the citrus and floral notes that were distinctly Mia.

"Are you sure you want to dance?" Mia giggled when Eliza began tracing kisses along Mia's shoulder. "We do have an entire private suite two floors up. I can think of a million things I want to do to you."

"Later," Eliza murmured. "I'm right where I want to be."

"Good," Mia said.

The song ended and another began. This one was faster and friends and family began filling the dance floor around them. Eliza was going to have to actually dance, not simply sway to the rhythm. Butterflies whirled to life in her stomach.

"You can do this," Mia whispered. She grabbed Eliza's chin and said, "Eyes right here, Brewer."

* * * * *

Get up to 4 Free

We'll send you 2 free books from each ser
PLUS a free Mystery Gift.

FREE Value Over **$25**

Both the **Harlequin® Historical** and **Harlequin® Romance** series feat
compelling novels filled with emotion and simmering romance.

YES! Please send me 2 FREE novels from the Harlequin Historical or Harlequin R
series and my FREE Mystery Gift (gift is worth about $10 retail). After receiving them,
wish to receive any more books, I can return the shipping statement marked "cancel."
cancel, I will receive 5 brand-new Harlequin Historical books every month and be bill
$6.39 each in the U.S. or $7.19 each in Canada, or 4 brand-new Harlequin Romance L
Print books every month and be billed just $7.19 each in the U.S. or $7.99 each in Cana
savings of 20% off the cover price. It's quite a bargain! Shipping and handling is just 50¢
book in the U.S. and $1.25 per book in Canada.* I understand that accepting the 2 free bo
and gift places me under no obligation to buy anything. I can always return a shipment a
cancel at any time by calling the number below. The free books and gift are mine to keep
matter what I decide.

Choose one: ☐ **Harlequin Historical** (246/349 BPA G36Y)   ☐ **Harlequin Romance Larger-Print** (119/319 BPA G36Y)   ☐ **Or Try Both!** (246/349 & 119/319 BPA G36Z)

Name (please print) _____

Address _____ Apt. # ____

City _____ State/Province _____ Zip/Postal Code _____

Email: Please check this box ☐ if you would like to receive newsletters and promotional emails from Harlequin Enterprises ULC and its affiliates. You can unsubscribe anytime.

Mail to the Harlequin Reader Service:
IN U.S.A.: P.O. Box 1341, Buffalo, NY 14240-8531
IN CANADA: P.O. Box 603, Fort Erie, Ontario L2A 5X3

Want to explore our other series or interested in ebooks? Visit www.ReaderService.com or call 1-800-873-8635.

*Terms and prices subject to change without notice. Prices do not include sales taxes, which will be charged (if applicable) based on your state or country of residence. Canadian residents will be charged applicable taxes. Offer not valid in Quebec. This offer is limited to one order per household. Books received may not be as shown. Not valid for current subscribers to the Harlequin Historical or Harlequin Romance series. All orders subject to approval. Credit or debit balances in a customer's account(s) may be offset by any other outstanding balance owed by or to the customer. Please allow 4 to 6 weeks for delivery. Offer available while quantities last.

Your Privacy—Your information is being collected by Harlequin Enterprises ULC, operating as Harlequin Reader Service. For a complete summary of the information we collect, how we use this information and to whom it is disclosed, please visit our privacy notice located at https://corporate.harlequin.com/privacy-notice. Notice to California Residents – Under California law, you have specific rights to control and access your data. For more information on these rights and how to exercise them, visit https://corporate.harlequin.com/california-privacy. For additional information for residents of other U.S. states that provide their residents with certain rights with respect to personal data, visit https://corporate.harlequin.com/other-state-residents-privacy-rights/.

HHHRLP25